T0322942

The Gentleman from Peru

ANDRÉ ACIMAN

The Gentleman from Peru

faber

First published in 2024
by Faber & Faber Ltd
The Bindery, 51 Hatton Garden
London EC1N 8HN

Typeset by Faber & Faber Ltd
Printed in the UK by CPI Group (UK) Ltd, Croydon, CR0 4YY

A CIP record for this book
is available from the British Library

ISBN 978–0–571–38511–9

Printed and bound in the UK on FSC® certified paper in line with our continuing
commitment to ethical business practices, sustainability and the environment.
For further information see faber.co.uk/environmental-policy

2 4 6 8 10 9 7 5 3

For Antonio and Carla Sersale

CHILDERM

CHAPTER ONE

'Perhaps this might help,' said the stranger. He walked over to their table and touched Mark on the shoulder. 'Just breathe deeply and count to five.'

They'd been seeing him for at least three days, sitting across from them at a corner table in the hotel's dining area by the pool. Always keeping to himself, occasionally exchanging a few short pleasantries with the tall, white-haired waiter, otherwise very quiet and reserved.

Though he always sat alone, he never brought anything to read with him – just a green Moleskine notebook, which he kept open upside down like a diminutive camping tent, a tiny black, clipless fountain pen, and a pair of glasses, which he tossed on the table with total disregard for how they landed on the tablecloth, as though still denying that he needed them. He was in his early sixties, looked dapper, slim, and always buoyant in his well-pressed, double-breasted navy seersucker jacket, a linen shirt, and silver-grey tie, topped by a vibrant-coloured pocket square.

They had spotted him a few times in the lobby or on the long terrace and had begun wondering about him, probably thinking he was another one of those stereotypical semi-retired Italian gentlemen who'd done well for themselves and who pick a spa in the hills or a beach resort where they vacation, socialize a bit, play bridge at night, and for a few weeks manage to stay away from their wives, their mistresses and grandchildren. But this gentleman didn't socialize, didn't play bridge, hadn't come for the waters or the mud baths, and unlike the other hotel guests kept asking the waiters to lower the volume of the already muted Vivaldi music piped into the dining area. Once, on heading to what was usually his table, he had thrown a glance in their direction, even given them an imperceptible bow as a passing salutation; but he never uttered a word. They did not return his greeting, feeling that his old-world manner was too chilly and formal for them to know exactly how to respond. Their eyes had simply cast a blank, bewildered stare on his figure, ignoring his distant salutation and trying not to encourage what he might be up to next. 'I'm telling you, he's been studying us,' said one of them. 'Weird,' agreed another.

Their table was the busiest and largest in the hotel dining area and occupied the space lining a good portion of the balustrade overlooking the beach and the marina on the left. As soon as they'd shown up the first few times, the waiters had hastily joined together three tables and thrown a long tablecloth over them. Later, after they'd all finished eating and left, the waiters would remove the long tablecloth, crumple it up, and separate the tables again. Eventually, seeing that the cohort never went elsewhere for breakfast or dinner, the waiters decided to leave the tables joined together for the remainder of their stay. They were not the only Americans in the hotel, but the youngest and the loudest. When the two guitarists came round to their table in the evening, the women in their group would suddenly beam, turn to face the players, and laugh aloud as they attempted to hum along with the music. Everyone else in the hotel spoke softly, ate very slowly, and drank far less. The young Americans were the last to leave at night, and, by the time they'd ordered dessert, all the other tables were already being set up for breakfast.

After dinner, most of the ageing hotel guests liked to spend their time either in the common area not far from the lobby or playing bridge in the card room. For them, this was not a resort where you came for a few days but where you spent at least three weeks in the hotel and stayed put there, socializing with other guests who'd been coming here for years if not decades, and touring the environs a bit only to return for a short swim, then light cocktails and a splendid dinner. The chef, as the hotel staff kept reminding the young *Signori Americani*, was world famous and the author of three bestselling cookbooks. After dinner, the much older folk would sip mineral water or chamomile on the veranda or, fearing draughts, would eventually repair to the tea room. They were dubbed 'the knitting pool' by the young Americans, because two of the eldest women were frequently seen knitting, while the men who later seemed eager to move to the patio to discuss the sorry state of Italian politics would sit in groups of threes and fours before turning in when it got a tad chilly. After dinner, the young Americans liked to crowd into the small bar area that probably housed more gins and single malts than any luxury bar in the United Kingdom.

'I wonder if the ladies play gin rummy after napping in the afternoon,' said Margot, one of the Americans who worked in an art gallery and was seldom reluctant to crack a snarky remark about people she didn't know. Everyone laughed. 'Yes, but do you know what happens to their husbands?' asked Oscar, who was a Chilean schooled in the United States and had a savage sense of humour. He waited a while for someone to hazard an answer, and seeing no one did, couldn't help but elicit the old joke about why such husbands invariably died first. 'Why do they die first?' asked Margot, yanking off his sailor's cap and dropping it on her head. 'Because they want to die,' he answered.

The group burst out laughing again. Margot stared at the two eldest ladies, who had been discussing knitting stitches, and smiled a vague, long-distance smile at them. 'Just promise to shoot me if I end up knitting in a hotel drinking overheated chamomile when I am eighty.' And with this she gave Oscar his sailor's cap again but, to tease him, tilted the visor to his left. He readjusted the cap, but she struggled to turn its visor to his right this time. 'Old people live way too long,' she said, letting go of the hat.

The two pensioners didn't know they were the butt of so much humour, and, catching smiles on the young Americans from across the dining area, exchanged subdued smiles with them. 'They're waking up,' said Margot. 'Mustn't rouse the old ducks.'

'You're being mean again,' said Mark, who was the voice of reason in the group.

Margot caught herself, was quiet at first, then

8

staring straight back at him said, 'I know.' But then, seeing no one had said anything, she added, 'I was just thinking of my grandmother who was lucky enough to die in her sleep. I want to be spared getting old.'

'Still,' Mark continued, 'you shouldn't say things like that. I lost my granny a few weeks ago, and I loved her.' Mark always wore one piece of tennis gear or another even when he wasn't playing. Now, because of a recent injury, he was continually rubbing his shoulder.

The well-dressed gentleman, however, stood out from everyone else in the hotel and seemed perfectly content to be left alone. Paul, who worked in DC for a congressman, had run into the man in the airy hotel lobby and, without knowing why, had greeted him with a non-committal smile that he couldn't retract in time. The gentleman had made a perfunctory nod but hadn't smiled. 'He just hates us,' said Mark.

'Could be a hired assassin type living off the fat of his Swiss bank account,' said Margot.

'No, an assassin on his last job.'

'Who is he killing?'

'Maybe one of us,' said Paul.

'I see him as a painter,' said Angelica, who always came to the dining area already wearing a bathing suit and a translucent wraparound.

'Maybe.'

'He's too old-school to be an artist.'

'Gives me the heebie-jeebies,' said Margot.

After breakfast the gentleman would leave as quietly as he had entered. 'Probably meeting his mole.'

'Mossad.'

'Why Mossad?'

'Looks Jewish and far too slick for someone born into wealth. There's something fishy about him.'

'You're being mean again, Margot.'

After dinner the gentleman liked to sit on the veranda by himself and smoke a cigarette, sometimes two.

On their third night they watched him do something totally unusual. He had gone back inside, changed into his bathing suit, and walked down the stairs leading to the beach where he started swimming all alone in the dark. The Americans never saw him come back up the stairs.

'I can just see it in the papers: *Ex-assassin takes his own life.*'

'Stop it, already.'

'I wonder what his deal is.'

They agreed that none of them understood him. But then they never gave him much thought and inevitably forgot about him. All they seemed to care about was enjoying the hotel and the surrounding beach. By daylight they liked to go swimming and boating; they spent long hours at breakfast, lunch and dinner, and in the evening, after a stint at the hotel bar, they liked to go partying at one of the various night clubs around the hills.

At first, no one could tell why he had walked over to their table or why he was aiming straight for Mark. But before anyone knew what was happening, he had placed his palm on Mark's right shoulder, did not apologize for intruding, did not ask permission, didn't even hesitate to make what was clearly an invasive gesture. Instead, he spoke his few words with the effortless ease and authority of someone who'd done it many times before. 'Perhaps this might help,' he said.

Stunned by the move, everyone at their table gaped as the gentleman, who was diminutive by comparison to the athlete, said, 'No, don't move yet, just give it a few seconds.' And then immediately started the countdown 'Five, four, three, two, one' – after which he slowly removed his hand. 'The pain should be gone now.'

Mark, who had been writhing in pain since his shoulder injury, was so startled by the appearance of the white-bearded stranger in the navy-blue sports jacket that he did not know how to react or what to say. But moments later, 'I can't believe it,' he said, standing up. Everyone thought he was about to shove the stranger aside or hit him across the face. Instead, he reached for his right shoulder with his left hand, and kept groping the area around it as if trying to see whether the pain had indeed vanished or moved elsewhere. 'I can't feel any pain, it's just not there,' he repeated with total disbelief. He continued to twist himself around to check his neck, his back, the back of his skull, still trying to determine how the pain, which had been crippling him for days, had slipped away in a matter of seconds simply because the stranger in the navy jacket had taken the liberty of placing a hand to his shoulder and counted down the seconds.

'But where did the pain go?' he asked, turning to his friends, as though they'd know any more than he did. He was still startled and kept looking around and behind him as though someone had filched his wallet and was about to toss it over to another guest as a practical joke. For a moment he seemed to be asking the man who had healed him to put the pain back where it belonged.

But the pain wasn't there.

'Pain's like a sneaky reptile,' said the stranger. 'It appears on its own, inhabits your body for as long as it chooses, sometimes forever, and, if you're lucky, it sneaks away without saying goodbye.'

For a moment it seemed to Mark that he was being used as an unwitting prop in a party trick. Someone pretends to guess the card you picked, but you know it's a trick. He'll slice a woman in two, but you've seen it done many times. He pulls coins from behind your ear and you laugh like a three-year-old, though you suspect it's a sham. Sometimes someone will hypnotize you and make you say things in public you wouldn't dare whisper to yourself but all along you know it's bogus. On a rare occasion a magician will explain his trick to his public and just when everyone thought they got it and couldn't wait to perform it on someone else, lo and behold, the explanation turns out to be a party trick as well – and you're no wiser than you were at the beginning of the show.

But this was real. As the man said: the pain didn't even bother saying goodbye. 'So, it's like gone, gone?' Mark asked. 'Or will I find it at the count of three?'

The stranger looked at him with a patronizing smile the way Jesus might have looked at Lazarus after raising him from the dead, meaning *Have faith, brother, you're good to go.*

'And I can throw away all the meds everyone made me buy these past few weeks?'

'For all you know, you can flush them down the toilet,' the stranger said, with an almost amused snicker in his voice. 'You'll be fine, trust me.'

'And you do this for . . . free?' Mark asked, already worried at being presented with a bill.

'Totally for free,' echoed the gentleman. 'On the house.'

'No second visit?' Mark finally asked, meaning to inject humour so as not to look totally humbled by the experience.

'No second visit.'

'So, this is it, then?' an incredulous Mark continued.

'This is it.'

'Seriously?'

The older man looked at Mark with quizzical

eyes. 'Look, I'm no soapbox huckster and this was not a magic show,' he finally said in flawless Oxonian English that bore the faintest trace of a Hispanic accent. 'It was obvious from my table that you were in pain, I could see you writhing and stiffening, and I wanted to make it go away. That's all. I promise.'

Sensing the heavy silence that had fallen between them, the stranger seemed about to click his heels, withdraw and go back to his table, when Mark invited him to join them for a glass of wine and dessert. He had meant to add a few words of thanks, but the stranger hushed him with a gesture and simply said 'With pleasure' to the invitation. They squeezed together to make room for an extra chair, which the tall waiter brought to their table. 'It will be my second glass of wine and dessert. I try not to have more than one a day.' He asked them what had brought them to this place.

The question made almost all of them laugh, as they looked around the table to see who was going to tell their story. 'We were invited,' said

Basil, a lawyer in a large firm specializing in mergers, 'by a friend who rented the boat we sailed on. But at the last minute he had to stay in New York and wasn't able to come with us to Lisbon. So the boat picked us up in Lisbon and we've been sailing since, hoping to meet up with him at some point.'

'But why here?' asked the stranger.

'Apparently there's engine trouble, which is why we had to stop. The mechanics said they are working on repairs, but frankly, being here, in this hotel, with this beach and everything paid for, is beyond amazing. I, for one, don't care how long the repairs take.'

'Agreed,' said Emma. 'Engine trouble or not, I'm seriously tempted to unpack my things, settle here, and live the rest of my life with my paintbrushes, canvasses, beautiful views and be as far away from New York and every male of our species.' Then, after a pause, 'I am Emma,' she said.

'You look like such fast friends on a splendid private cruise.' He envied their camaraderie, he said.

'Well, we all graduated from college ten years ago. We made a vow.'

'What vow?'

'That the first to get rich would rent a boat and invite the others on a cruise. None of us made millions, but Malcolm did and he made good on his promise.'

'Except he isn't with you because of work.'

'Except he isn't with us because of work,' echoed Angelica, with a wry inflection in her voice as if reproaching him for being far too devoted to his millions when there were other, better things in life. 'But tell us who you are,' she asked.

'My name is Raúl.' A round of introductions and handshakes followed. Mark, Basil, Emma, Claire, Angelica, Paul, Margot and Oscar. They were eight at their table, so Basil was sure that Raúl wouldn't remember their names. But Raúl shook hands with everyone with a show of paying attention to each name. How long had he been

staying here? Mark asked. Ten days. Where was
he from? Originally, Peru, but he had studied
in England and France as well as in the United
States. Was this his first time here? No. He'd been
coming here almost every summer since his earli-
est childhood. He still owned a house on the hill
but never slept there, as it was leased to a family
friend. Where was he off to next? Back to France,
he told them. 'But I'm somewhat attached to this
place,' he explained.

'Somewhat attached?' quipped Margot, echoing
his words. 'What does that mean, exactly? Either
you are or aren't attached to it.'

Raúl turned to her and smiled broadly, almost
amused at the gratuitous dig. 'I suppose more
attached to it than I might care to claim.' He didn't
seem to mind being riled, and Margot had a mirth-
ful way about her that could pry open impacted
doors.

'Why more attached than you might care to
claim?' asked a perplexed Margot who echoed his
words but, hearing vagueness in what the man said,

was pouncing on every opportunity to get him to say what he meant.

'Don't pay attention to her manner,' interrupted Emma, 'she can't rein it in once she starts. She's just playing with you.'

'I like that. It might make me tell more than I normally like to tell a perfect stranger.'

'I'm not perfect,' Margot snapped. 'Anyone will tell you that.'

He looked at her, smiled once more, said nothing at first, then quietly added, 'But you are perfect. And you know it too. Though you may be wrong about one thing.'

'How so?'

'You're not a stranger.' By the sudden expression on her face, he must have sensed that his words had baffled her.

'So, why aren't we strangers?' she asked with a nervous, undecided smile. She was, as her expression suggested, giving him all the rope needed to hang himself. 'You've been watching us for days now. So, obviously, you might know a few things about us.'

'That's not why we aren't strangers.'

Margot's shoulders stiffened. 'So, let's hear it,' she said, staring at him with a goading smile.

'You two are having fun, I can tell,' said Oscar. 'When was the last time we saw Margot smile?'

'She never smiles,' said Mark.

'I wasn't smiling,' she protested.

There was a pause. The gentleman asked for a second glass of wine. 'It will be my third,' he said, almost as though admitting to a weakness. 'A terrible precedent.' Then after a pause, 'Your name is Marya,' he threw in.

'My name is Margot.' She was snapping at him now.

'Yes, but I could have sworn Marya was your birth name.'

'Why?'

'If you ask it's because you already know the answer.'

She looked at him with rising displeasure, as if deciding to contain her temper. 'My mother had wanted to name me Marya but my father wanted

Margaret, so they settled on Margot. But nobody knows this. How could you possibly have known – did you know her, did you know my mother?' She sounded irked and angry, as though ready to go to battle.

'I know many things about all of you.'

'Oh? Name some!' said Margot.

'I will tell you. But on one condition. First, may I have a slice of the cassata? It's very good, which is why I never order it.'

Basil signalled to the waiter.

'So, what is it that you know?' Margot asked.

Raúl took a hasty sip from his glass. This is when, turning to Mark, and holding the refilled wine glass lightly between two fingers, he uttered one word only: 'Twenty-two.'

Mark looked at him quizzically. 'What about twenty-two?' he asked.

'You know exactly,' replied Raúl.

Mark had no idea what. But then it hit him. 'You looked me up at the front desk!' he exclaimed.

'No, I didn't. But it is January twenty-second,

isn't it?' Mark looked around the table and began to feel as hollow and transparent as the near-emptied bottle of wine standing in the glass bucket next to him. But for his shoulder he would have dismissed the whole thing. He didn't believe in the super-natural, couldn't stand anyone who did, and the air of uplifted piety of those who speak of auras and astral houses brought out the worst in him. Now he was no longer sure.

Raúl looked around the table. 'I can tell, for example, that you were born in May,' he said to Claire. 'And the two of you were born in August,' he told Angelica and Paul, 'which says a lot. And you,' he said, turning to Basil, 'are November.'

Silence. He told the remaining two sitting at the table the month of their birth. No one disagreed.

'You left me out,' said Margot.

'I know.'

'Well?'

'You're born in a leap year, are you not?' he said, turning to Margot. 'Do you like twenty-ninth of February or first of March? Your pick.'

She looked totally dumbstruck.

'Let's drink to that,' said Basil, turning to the waiter who had just opened another bottle to replace the empty one in the bucket.

'You looked us up online,' said Basil. 'The easiest trick in the book.'

'No, I didn't,' said the gentleman from Peru. 'So let me turn to you, Basil,' he added with a tone that had lost all humour. 'You had a twin brother but he died *in utero* and by the time you were born there wasn't a trace of him left.'

'This is total nonsense,' said Basil, trying to contain himself and remain cordial with the gentleman. Then, with a glint of irony on his features: 'Are you suggesting I cannibalized my twin brother?'

'Happens more often than you think.'

'This is totally freaky,' said Mark.

'If you don't believe me, please text your mother in New Orleans right now and ask if she had expected twins.'

'How did you know she lives in New Orleans?'

Without looking at Basil, Raúl simply stared at

his empty glass and said, 'I just know.'

'How could you possibly know about twins?' asked Basil. 'Did you have access to hospital records? Unless you knew my mother, or her gynaecologist, or whatever.'

'I don't like rummaging into family secrets. So, let's stay with the missing twin,' said Raúl.

Meanwhile, Basil had taken out his phone and began texting the question to his mother. 'We'll see what she says,' he said, still shaking his head at the absurdity of the question he had just asked his mother.

'I already know what she'll say,' said Raúl.

'Oh, don't listen to him,' said Margot, fidgeting in her seat and looking more vexed by the minute. 'This whole thing is one big hoax, Basil. He looked us up online. He's probably the hotel magician, hustler and con artist who comes with breakfast, free Wi-Fi and cable TV.' She looked at Mark. 'Was the shoulder cure a hoax as well?'

'Well, maybe it's a placebo effect,' interjected Mark, 'but, to be honest, the pain did go away.'

'If you believe I'm a swindler, let me be more specific.' And turning to Emma, Raúl said: 'You lost someone two months ago.'

'I did.'

'You'd borrowed but never returned his watch.'

'Yes.'

'The reversible watch with the blue face.'

'That's correct.'

'And the man was your father.'

Totally stunned, Emma sat still. Her chin was quivering and she was clearly on the verge of tears. 'I kept it because I knew he was dying and I didn't want it left in the house with all the visiting nurses around. In my absurd moments, I kept hoping to return it to him if he got better. But how do you know all this?'

'I'll explain later. But I couldn't have looked it up, could I?' he said, turning to Margot, who for some reason seemed even more flustered as she leant forward, looked around the table, and finally stood up, saying, 'I think I'll go for a walk.'

Raúl raised his head and looked at her. 'Don't go yet. Please.'

She did not reply and simply rammed her chair back to the table. It made a loud noise. But then she stood bolted to the spot.

Meanwhile, 'Here it is,' said Basil, who had just that moment received a text from his mother in New Orleans.

'And what does your mother say?' asked Margot.

Basil stared at Raúl. 'You were right. Apparently, they had suspected twins but only one child was born. But my mother asked how did I know this, and honestly, I don't know what to tell her.'

'Tell her nothing.'

'This is becoming really ugly,' exclaimed Margot and, in a huff, she scuttled out of the dining area.

'I think I must have upset her,' said Raúl as he turned, looking surprised. 'With Margot, one never knows.'

'So, I'll enjoy this last drop of wine and head back to my room,' he added. Yet he was staring at Angelica and Paul. 'You are not married, are you?'

Paul seemed startled by the question, and hesitated before answering. 'I'm not. She is. I thought you knew everything,' came his little dig.

'Here is what I do know. You were in love in college, weren't you? Yet neither of you ever did anything about it. No one knew. You yourselves didn't know, or didn't want to know, and have been struggling not to know it ever since, even now, among your friends at this very table. Am I right so far?'

Paul looked over at Angelica, smiled uneasily, and turning to her, said, 'He may have a point.'

Angelica did not respond right away. 'Could be,' she said, but was quiet again, and then, speaking softly and smiling awkwardly as if trying to make light of what had just been said: 'Do you think Raúl's onto us, just maybe, maybe?'

'Why, have I spoken out of turn?' asked a baffled Raúl.

'Nah. We've known for years,' intervened Basil. 'Everyone here suspected. How long did it take for this to come out?'

'Just ten years,' said a humbled Paul.

'Feels like fifty to us,' said Oscar, laughing.

'Actually,' said Raúl, 'it took three centuries.'

'Any more stunning revelations in your bag of tricks, old man?' asked Oscar.

Raúl did not say anything. He just stood up. 'Enough magic for one round,' he said, and politely pushed back his seat without making a sound.

CHAPTER TWO

The next evening the group of young Americans walked into the dining area just about when everyone else in the hotel was finishing dessert. Raúl, as always, was starting his second course by himself. As soon as the Americans spotted him, they greeted him. Mark even patted him on the back with a jovial, hail-fellow, semi-patronizing gesture meant both to express his abiding gratitude and to erase the pitiable figure he must have cut the day before as the injured athlete of the group. They asked if he would like to join them for drinks at the hotel pub after he was done with dinner. With pleasure, replied the gentleman from Peru.

They had planned on going to one of the clubs around the hill, but had eventually decided to stay put on the hotel grounds. 'You'll be our guest. Or, rather, Malcolm's guest. We've told him about you – he's sorry he couldn't be here to meet you.'

Raúl gave the invitation to the bar table some thought, almost as though he regretted having accepted so readily and should have reconsidered. Then he added: 'Tell Malcolm to beware of any last-minute transaction before the markets close today. He may not be able to avert or reverse its course, but he can certainly take provisions by hedging against the risks. Don't forget.'

Basil made an it's-been-duly-noted gesture, but Raúl, pointing his fork at him, insisted: 'Tell him now, as in this minute.'

'Now, as in now?'

'Exactly,' said Raúl. 'Call him!'

'He's involved in crazy ventures,' Raúl explained to those around him, 'but I know that this one is dangerous and he needs to sell before the markets close today.'

The call was made. It lasted no more than a few seconds. Angelica grabbed the phone and told him she missed him. He missed her too.

'Malcolm thanks you,' she told Raúl a moment later.

Later in the evening, as they gathered in the tiny pub and ordered drinks, Mark remarked that if Raúl was so good at forecasting volatile shifts in the market, why hadn't his skills helped him make a fortune himself?

'Because I know nothing about the markets. Besides, I'm always afraid of risking the funds my good parents left me. I often know what dangers lie in store or what people are planning or plotting to do. But I've been tragically blind in the past – the greatest catastrophe in my life caught me totally by surprise. There've been other, terrible instances where my predictions simply proved totally wrong. But birthdays and past events are not difficult for me. Still, I know something is afoot in New York today. You watch: something will happen just before the market closes in half an hour.'

As they were relishing their drinks, Raúl told them he'd take them to see something special in the coming days if they had nothing better to do. Had any of them read the *Aeneid*?

Many of them had read bits and pieces. 'Courtesy of our liberal arts education which cost our parents a fortune,' said Oscar, 'and yet it all boils down to bits and pieces. Which is why we know nothing.'

'Exactly,' said Margot.

'They taught us contemporary poetry and contemporary issues, even contemporary grammar. But ultimately, like Margot says, nothing,' said Oscar.

'*Like* Margot says?' she asked, making fun of him. '*As* Margot says. *Apologizomai.*'

Everyone laughed. 'Courtesy of college Greek 101.'

All toasted their alma mater.

Raúl didn't quite understand why they were laughing but let the matter pass. He simply added that, if they wanted, he would take them to where Cuma was, one of the spots where Aeneas stopped on his travels after leaving Carthage. There, incidentally, lies the entrance to Avernus, the doorway to the world of the dead, on Lake Avernus.

'Have you been there?' asked Margot.

'Yes. But never alone.'

'Why? I'd like to go,' said Paul.

'Me too,' said Angelica.

'It's the kind of thing Fellini would have loved, a group of friends working their way down a craggy passage into the underworld where we're told Styx, the sacred river, ran. There you'll see the mourning fields, the *Lugentes campi*,' explained Raúl. 'This is where all broken hearts tell their woebegone tales of love to anyone who passes by and cares to stop to listen: Phaedra, who took her own life for loving her stepson after she opened up her heart to him; Dido, who lit a fire and threw herself into it while Aeneas watched her burn from aboard his ship to Italy; Procris, who was mistakenly speared by her lover, and poor Caenis, raped by a god and begging to be turned into a man so as never to be raped again. Haven't you all been burnt and speared and raped in your hearts at least once?'

'No comment,' said Oscar, which made everyone burst out laughing. But no one answered.

'Which means all of you have,' said Raúl.

37

'Everyone's been hurt. But I still can't believe that people actually take their own lives for love. It's so kitsch, so camp.'

That was Margot.

'I almost did once. At least I thought of it very, very seriously,' said Emma. 'But I wasn't going to do it with violence or with pills, so I decided to starve myself. And I almost did. Then one day I saw someone eating country bread with triple-cream cheese and drinking a glass of red, and I said: *Enough!*'

'It would be just like Emma to be saved by cheese,' said Oscar.

'Not for me either the Lugentes fields,' interrupted Claire, the quiet one who was a teacher, 'even though I spent two years on those fields obsessing over a woman who'll never know how much I ached for her.'

'Marisol? Are we back to Marisol? Why am I not surprised? Claire, get over it, please, you've been bellyaching for years.'

That was Margot again.

But Claire didn't seem to hear Margot.

'We always know when someone loves us, even when we don't want their love. Marisol knows,' said Claire. 'I know she knows.'

'And what about you, Raúl? Have you crossed the *Lugentes campi*?' Claire asked Raúl.

Raúl did not answer right away. But then: 'Yes, I have. We never recover. Whoever bruised us left a mark that stays there forever. Do we ever recover from our parents? Or from the cruelty of our first arithmetic teacher? Or from someone loved in adolescence? You may seek to recover, and many of us are persuaded we have, until we realize that if we commit the same mistakes time and time again, it's not because we keep choosing the wrong partner or because we don't know how to love, but because new loves won't help us heal from that one ancient wound. All new love can do is mask the wound – and for some, this is good enough.'

'Did someone hurt you that much?' asked Margot.

'Yes, once. But only once.'

'And?'

'I never discuss it.'

'Which tells us you've never recovered,' said Margot, clearly pleased to score a point at the expense of the gentleman from Peru.

'It was fate that hurt me, not her. But back to Avernus,' he said, clearly trying to change the subject; 'if you visit the site of the entrance to the underworld you'll see where dead souls shamble about complaining of this and that, some with remorse in their hearts, others with regrets, each waiting to be called up to have a say on who they'll want to be once they're brought back to life, not realizing why most keep making the wrong choice each time they're alive again. We come back to correct our lives, because most lives are lived imperfectly.'

'Why do they keep making the wrong choice?'

'Why? Because no one wants to accept who they truly are. Everyone requests the self they believe is the very best, hoping to be loved for who they're not and could never be. And the tiny miracle of life, the tiniest yet most imponderable miracle, is when we stumble on people who see us for who we are and want us just for who we are – and these are the ones we spurn the most, the ones we let into our lives with resentment, scorn and boundless apathy, sometimes even with hatred. But the moment two individuals love each other for who each truly is then time for them stops, and if these two don't die together, then the partner who lives on never recovers, never forgets, and keeps waiting until they meet again in who knows how many lifetimes. In Shakespeare's own words, *either is the other's mine.* The beloved always comes back. Always will. But the wait is excruciating – they wait not just to live together but also to die together. You see, it's life that is provisional, not love.' The group sat stupefied by Raúl's words.

'What I'd love to do is invite all of you tomorrow morning to the bubbling sulphur craters of Pozzuoli near which, we're told, Aeneas went into the underworld and where Ulysses spoke to dead Achilles and then, without warning, suddenly ran into his mother and said, "Did you die then too, mother?" and thereupon tried to embrace her three times, and three times clutched just air.

'Haven't we all embraced air when all we wanted was to hold someone dear to us when they were gone from our lives? We too become air, you know. And just think of all the people we'll never know exist but who embrace us each and every night in their fantasy lives. We're air to them no less than we are air to those we love in secret.'

'You make the underworld sound so very real. Is there really such a place?' asked Paul.

'It's in Homer.'

'And he never ever lies,' said Margot. 'You're pulling my leg. I can tell.' She smiled.

Meanwhile, the waiter came to deliver another round of drinks, and a sudden whiff of something rose from their martinis and filled the tiny room.

'What's that incredible smell?' Basil asked.

'It's just the lemons that grow on the Amalfi coast,' said Raúl. 'Nothing like them in the world. You don't know what lemon really is until you taste these.'

'Here,' said Raúl, calling the waiter back and asking him to bring a fresh lemon with a paring knife.

The waiter did as he was asked, and returned with a shiny lemon plus a small, sharp knife.

Raúl held the lemon in his left hand and began to carve out pieces of the rind, which he distributed to Paul and Angelica, then to Basil, and then to every one of those present, including three tourists who happened to overhear Raúl's effusive elegy on lemons.

'Have you ever smelt lemons like this?' he asked.

'No, never,' came the choral response.

Margot was the last to be given a piece of the rind, and was almost unwilling to take it from Raúl's hand.

'It won't kill you,' he said, realizing she was reluctant to have anything to do with lemons – or with him. Yet he did not seem to mind her ill-concealed hostility. She took one sniff then dropped the rind into the nearest ashtray.

Everyone kept smelling their little sliver of rind, without letting go.

'Now you know why I need to return to Italy every year,' said Raúl.

'To smell the rind of a lemon?' Typical Margot sarcasm.

'You may be right,' said Raúl. 'Sometimes the best things couldn't be simpler: the scent of lemon, a few bars from a Beethoven quartet, the shiny broad shoulder of a woman in a bathing suit resting on a beach towel, a seascape by Dufy, or just the smile on someone's face you love.'

'Can we add Caol Ila from Scotland to the list?'

'And olives from Greece.'

'Or mangoes from India?'

'Foie gras from France.'

'And five golden rings!' rang Oscar's voice. Everyone burst out laughing.

Then, from nowhere, one of them asked, 'When did you learn how to heal people?'

Raúl smiled, as though already sensing that the question, seemingly harmless, was only the opening volley to more questions.

'I don't know exactly, but when I look back, I

probably learnt by getting hurt myself and applying a hand to my hurt knee. Everyone instinctively touches that part of our body when we've banged it against something. So, I touched my knee. Five seconds after I'd touched it, the pain went away. I thought everyone did so. When I played with children my age, whenever someone hurt himself in the park or the sandbox, they'd immediately place a hand where they hurt. One day I saw a child touch his hurt knee, but his pain wasn't going away and he was crying. So, I literally gave him a hand. And right away his pain was gone.

'He told his mother. I expected the mother to rush to thank me profusely – instead, she warned me never to touch her son again. "*Niente stregonerie, capisci!*" she said, meaning I was a witch. I was convinced I'd done something terribly wrong. From then on, each time someone was hurt, I'd leave them alone, and would watch them suffer.

'When my mother had a kidney stone and woke up one night in terrible agony, I asked her if she could point to the spot where the pain was. She indicated her waist and the back of her kidney, she couldn't even locate the source of pain around her midriff. I asked her to place my hand on the spot itself, but I didn't want her to know why I was asking, for fear she too would think me a witch. She took hold of my hand and placed it around where the pain radiated. And right away, within the count of a few seconds, the pain was gone. As was her kidney stone, which was tiny and which she passed a few hours later. I denied I had anything to do with it, but from that day on I knew. My mother never spoke about it. But I'm sure she knew. A few years later, when she had an infection on her foot, she asked if I could do something. And of course I did, with the same result.'

'How old were you at the time?'

'Seven. But I've known I had that gift since I was two, maybe even younger.'

'Do you even remember things as far back as that? No one remembers being three.'

Raúl looked down silently at his martini with the lemon rind floating in it and then stared at the rindless little lemon sitting bared and scarred next to the large bowl of peanuts. Everyone sitting in the bar area could sense that something serious had crossed his mind but that he was reluctant to discuss it.

'I go back,' he finally said, looking up, and holding his glass as if for sympathy and support, knowing that everyone's eyes were now riveted on him.

'You go back,' said Emma. And after a pause, 'What does that mean, *you go back*?'

Once again, Raúl looked down at his glass ruefully and was clearly trying to avoid giving explanations. Breaking a small piece from a breadstick that had come with the drinks, he put it into his mouth, as if it were a cigarette.

'This is making me nervous,' said Claire.

'Okay, one last question, and then I promise I'll stop,' said Emma.

'Go ahead,' he said, again with that guileful smile of someone who'd heard all of it so many, many times before. He picked up his paper napkin, wiped some of the condensation around the rim of his glass, and, satisfied with how the glass now looked, took a sip.

'What did you mean by *going back*?' Emma asked.

Again, he looked around the table. 'I don't want to upset anyone or make anyone uncomfortable, nor do I want to sound unnecessarily cryptic. But I'll answer this one question and then, please, can we move on to another subject?'

'Okay.'

'The point is we all go back. We spend more time than we know trying to go back. We call it fantasizing, we call it dreaming, we give it all manner of names. But we're all crawling back, each in his or her own way. Very few of us know the way, most never find the door, much less the key to the door. We're just groping in the dark. Some of us may even feel we're not from planet Earth but have come down from elsewhere and are all pretending to be normal earthlings. And yet not one of us is. We might as well come from Mars or, as happens to be my case, from a very distant place, or planet, called Peru, which may no longer even exist for me. Some know their way back and some won't ever know.'

'And which kind of earthling are you, then?' asked Margot who had obviously been listening and was no longer heeding the young man who had accosted her and had joined the clan in the bar.

'Sometimes I know the way.' Then seeing no one was reacting: 'And sometimes I can lead the way.'

'Wait, wait,' said Emma, 'what does *lead the way* mean?'

Suddenly Raúl looked serious. 'It means that I can take you back to places you knew long, long before.'

'Before what?' asked Emma, clearly growing very impatient.

'Before you were born. Even I could figure that one out,' blurted Margot.

But Raúl had read the situation correctly. After hearing such talk no one in the room could resist thinking of the questions they wished to ask, which explained the sudden silence as each hovered above him like an undecided bird circling the air before finally landing on its branch.

'Let me put it this way. All of us remember having had another self. Which could be a mirage, or a fleeting sense of someone we were long ago, perhaps elsewhere – call it a hinter-self who feels less transient than we'd like to believe. But here's the catch,' he said, stopping midway as if to collect his thoughts. He took another sip.

'And the catch is?' Margot asked, as if unable to stand the silence and determined to be testy, perhaps to prove once and for all that the gentleman from Peru was fabricating the whole thing.

'This other self of ours may not be a bygone self, but a self living elsewhere even as we're having drinks this very minute in this fabulous hotel.'

'You mean as in a parallel universe?'

'Call it what you will. But there may be more selves out there: some still unsprung, like tiny egg cells that haven't been fertilized; some already released; and some waiting for the end. Each one of us is a constellation of selves, some are not even lodged in us, but in other people, which is why sometimes we recognize others right away – because they are us in someone else's body.'

This time Raúl grabbed a few peanuts from the bowl and began to chew them ever so slowly.

'How many at this table have at least once called an old phone number that you knew was no longer yours?'

None of those present said they had, but all gave a startled giggle at the question.

'You didn't come out to say you tried, but you all laughed, which proves my point: you've all called an old phone number. And what do you tell the person who picks up the phone, if someone does pick up? Hello, I am an older you, greetings and salutations? Or it could be the other way around: I am the you you haven't quite become yet.

'Or let me ask a different question, then: how many have passed by an old apartment where you used to live once and then looked upstairs to see if the person you were back then still has his lights on?'

Startled giggles again.

'Exactly! And how many have sought out an old love to test if the old lover we once were was still alive in us, only to be totally surprised when we caught ourselves almost willing to start all over again with someone whose last name we couldn't for the life of us recall?'

No answer.

'We may no longer be the person we once were, but what if this person did not necessarily die but continued his life in the shadowland of our own, so that you could say that our life is filled with shadow-selves who continue to tag along and to beckon us in all directions even as we live our own lives – all these selves clamouring to have their say, their time, their life, if only we listened and gave in to them!

'What if we switch roles from time to time, and become the shadow-self of the person we were two minutes ago? And then sideline that new self moments later for a third or a fourth? What if we are no more than a perpetual three-card monte of reshuffled hinter-selves? We traffic in shadow-selves.

The old self, the new self, the shadow-self, self number seven or number eleven, the self we always knew we were but never became, the self we left behind and never recovered, the might-have-been self that couldn't be but might still be, though we both fear yet hope it might come along one day and rescue us from the person we've had to be all our years.

'But as I said, it's not just the past that haunts us. What haunts us with equal magnitude is what has not happened yet, for there are shadow-selves and shadow-lives waiting in the wings all the time. We are constantly reworking and reinventing both the past and the future. Sometimes we're in the street or in a crowded bus, and we just know: that one day this person whose glance we caught or whose path we just crossed is another version of someone we know we've loved before and have yet to love again. But that person could just as easily be us in another body. And the beauty of it is that they feel it just as much as we do. Is this other person us or is it someone destined for us whom we keep missing each lifetime? Us in others, isn't this the definition of love?'

Oscar was about to ask a question but then changed his mind and remained silent.

'So, let me close with this thought since I have your attention but may have bored all of you to death already. The important thing is not knowing that there is or that there was or that there might be another us somewhere. What matters, my friends, is making contact. *Only connect*. The most difficult thing on earth.

'Do you think it is an accident that your boat needed to stop here or that Mark's shoulder hurt or that we are all here having a truly lovely and unusual evening? Maybe, or maybe not. And on that note let us toast with another round of martinis. On me, this time.'

Then, suddenly remembering: 'Call Malcolm!'

'Wouldn't you already know what he did?' came Margot's snide remark.

'I do know. But I want everyone else here to hear it from him.'

Basil right away picked up his phone and dialled New York. When Malcolm answered, Basil put the phone on speaker mode: 'I don't know what made me take the advice of some loser type you guys just met at the beach, but just tell him that if I'd given him ten per cent of what I managed to rescue thanks to him, he'd be a millionaire.'

Raúl snickered at the words *loser type*. 'Tell him he owes me nothing and that I was only happy to help. But if he wishes, he could make a generous donation to a foundation for the deaf. A friend I loved was deaf . . .'

Malcolm overheard Raúl's voice and realized he had been put on speakerphone. 'Sorry, old man. And thanks so much. Got to run. Let me know if you have any other tips.'

Everyone was pleased to hear that Raúl had scored a victory.

'So, you go back?' asked Margot.

'So, I go back,' he replied.

'And can you take people with you?'

'You mean like a travel guide for time-travel tourists?'

'If you put it that way.'

'I have.'

'Whom would you take, if you had a choice?'

Raúl looked around the group of eight. 'I'd select Oscar.'

'Why me?'

'You'll see. Oscar needs to recall that he once lived in Antwerp and was named Christoffel Loewen,' began Raúl. 'Christoffel had a very sick mother who, despite her illness, lived a very long life, and as a result of needing constant tending night and day made it impossible for him to find a wife. Or so he wanted it rumoured. He could free himself for only two to three hours every day to pen letters for people who did not know how to write or who loved his handwriting and preferred to dictate them to him, but the rest of the time he read and wrote letters – letters to countless individuals in Europe, Russia, North and South America, always in flawless French, which he had learnt at school and mastered perfectly. He had a witty pen and everyone he wrote to always responded: writers, composers, philosophers, leaders, including Count Cavour,

Louis-Philippe, Empress Eugénie, Ivan Turgenev, Franz Liszt. When years later his mother died, he was already an old man whose sole passion by then was writing letters and amassing a huge stamp collection with their original letters and envelopes. The collection is priceless. A distant nephew got wind of the collection and, on inheriting all of Christoffel's property, would have sold it to a reputable dealer except that he died a few days before concluding the sale. No one knows of its existence.'

'Where is it?'

'It was left in an attic,' said Raúl.

'Is the building still there?'

'You mean, hasn't it burnt down yet or been bombed during the war? No, it hasn't.'

'Do you know the address, by any chance?' asked Oscar.

Raúl laughed.

'Yes, I do. I will give it to you. All you have to do when you show up at the door is say you are the grandson of Christoffel Loewen's nephew and have come to collect a package that was left for you. The old lady who owns the house and who knew the nephew won't be any trouble. You are, in my view, the rightful owner. With your gift of the gab I'm sure you'll charm her.'

Oscar was nonplussed, and didn't know whether to truly believe any of it.

'The important thing, as I said, is making contact. There are, as so many physicists will tell you, occasional openings between one time warp and another that are no wider than a sheet of onion paper. Then the slit shuts and you need to wait generations, centuries, who knows, millennia, for the next opportunity.'

'Will the visit be worth the trip?'

'Oh, yes,' said Raúl. 'It will change your life, and allow you to leave your job, pay off your college loans, and sail off with the young sailor who lent you his hat two nights ago.'

'You're terrifying,' said Oscar, bursting out laughing.

'I know,' smiled the gentleman from Peru, looking quite pleased with himself.

'I know you get this all the time, but would you do me a favour?' asked Angelica.

'What?'

'Tell us about us, about me and Paul?'

'Are you under the impression that yours is just love? Seriously, I've watched how you look at each other when the other isn't watching, and it's almost as if your life is in his life and his in yours. You've been friends since college and you've gone out with god knows how many others – you even got married to a very wealthy man whom you care for but have never and will never love. The decision on what to do is yours entirely. But if I know one thing from my own life, don't wait and don't give up, not now. Behind your love today there are entire lives of missed encounters and chance meetings. Once you lived in Baltimore and he in Mexico, and you met on a ship headed to, of all places, Anchorage. You both knew, knew right away. But one was in first class, the other in second, and you got off and he stayed on, and you never met again.

'Years and another lifetime later, he was a clerk

in a haberdashery and you walked in with your son trying to buy a present for your husband and once again the two of you knew, and neither dared. Does either of you remember the shop?'

Angelica and Paul stared at each other. 'No, we don't,' one of them said.

'Of course you don't. And yet—'

'—and yet?'

'The shop was in Helsinki almost abutting a wharf. Think of it together. I'll say no more.'

Raúl went on to tell them about the *Lugentes campi*, where all unfulfilled loves are parked, waiting, waiting, waiting.

'Most of us live our lives waiting for the right alignment. For this is what life is: a waiting room. But feel for the dead, who take what they've waited for to the underworld and continue waiting to come back to earth to be made to live again and wait some more. So, better one hour spent doing things we'll regret having done than a lifetime waiting for heaven to touch our lives.'

The wannabe lovers looked at each other like

teenagers fumbling with the facts of life, almost asking what they should do next. They remembered meeting the first time during registration in New England – but Helsinki, really? They remembered losing each other in school.

'I drifted away hoping you'd come looking for me, but you never did.'

'You drifted because you didn't want me to look for you.'

'And you met others.'

'You knew they were a sham.'

'Not after a while.'

'Why didn't you at least try?'

'I did try.'

'Not that I saw.'

'Did you think of her?' asked Raúl.

'All the time.'

'And did you know?' he asked Angelica.

'I did know but I stopped believing. He made such a secret of it. But there wasn't, and still isn't a single day when I don't catch myself hoping he thinks of me.'

Margot, who had been listening with Oscar, couldn't help but throw in: 'Helsinki! What were you doing in Helsinki in your previous life?'

'You're asking me? Ask him.'

The third round of drinks finally arrived and found everyone sitting down eager to ask Raúl about their own lives.

'Doesn't the passage of time make you sad, though?' asked Claire of Angelica. 'Living for the past ten years with someone who could be the wrong man – doesn't that bother you?'

'Yes. It makes me very sad. But what makes me sadder yet is that I may do nothing, despite Paul's admission, or mine. We may decide to lead the wrong life because we've gotten used to it.'

'No, no,' said Claire. 'Tonight feels almost like a midsummer night's dream. Spaces open up, errors are repaired, destinies untangled, and everything can be redressed.'

'Is this what this place is for you?' asked Raúl.

'Well, look at this bar. With the boat stopped, all of us have stepped out of time. Our troubles are

left behind, and our revels hardly started, something good is bound to occur.'

'And with this, ladies and gentlemen, I bid you
goodnight. Otherwise, tomorrow at sunrise we'll
all be quite a sight.'

CHAPTER THREE

For the next two days, Raúl totally disappeared.

And then, suddenly, there he was, as though he'd been there all along and the three who were coming barefoot up the uneven, ancient treads leading from the beach to the hotel had simply failed to notice him. Angelica, Margot and Emma. That morning, he was wearing a large straw hat, a pair of soiled shorts, a T-shirt that had seen better days, and was on his knees with a trowel in hand helping the gardener weed the edge of the stone-paved walk leading to the patio. When he saw them, he stood up, rubbed his dusty hand against his shorts, but sensing he was unable to rid it of dirt, withdrew it with a self-conscious smile.

'You disappeared,' said Margot.

'I had to go across to the island to sign some deeds and ended up spending the night there.'

He had a sunny disposition that morning and,

while staring at them, smiled many more times than he'd done over lunch the first time they had met.

'But here I was trying to finish this little stretch before lunch,' he said, surveying the work he'd done, and clearly not displeased with what he'd accomplished that day. 'I find this the best therapy in the world. You almost catch yourself talking to the ground, to these stones, to some of these weeds that I must uproot, and to the worms themselves whom you don't want to disturb, and frankly the silence is so intense and so magnificent. It's the pleasure people take in fishing, if you like fishing, which I hate. I love the heat when it's not so humid. And where are you people coming from?'

'We've just been swimming. Funny you should ask, though,' said Margot.

'Why?'

'I thought you knew everything – or had you forgotten?' The dart hit its mark.

'The weather was so wonderful, we lay on the beach then swam forever, up to the stationary barge,' said Angelica, clearly trying to ease out Margot's little dart.

Raúl adjusted his hat, almost looking for something to say, and finding nothing, looked at Margot.

'I think I've upset you, Margot.'

'You mean Marya,' she said with a sly look on her face, as though struggling to contain a smile.

'Now you're being cruel to me. I was just trying to apologize for the other day.'

'Accepted,' she replied.

Her answer had come so swiftly that Raúl saw it as both a perfunctory nod at his apology as well as an attempt to fend off formalities. He asked the three of them if they would join him for lunch at two. Emma said she was going back swimming, while Angelica said she was just about to have a very light snack with Paul.

'Why at two?' asked Margot.

'The dining area clears out a bit, and it gets quieter.'

'You mean after the young Americans leave the dining area and everyone else goes to nap?'

'Something like that.'

She pondered the invitation a tad longer than is usual. 'Accepted.'

'Will you allow me to order for the two of us now? I usually order what they catch earlier in the day.'

She looked at him and smiled. 'I said *accepted*.'

'Peace then?'

'We'll see about that.'

'Please say yes.'

Her smile was meant to convey a tepid alright, but he decided to take it as a categorical yes.

'Now I must get back to my weeding, otherwise the gardener will fire me.'

At two on the dot she arrived wearing a white linen blouse, baggy white linen trousers and a sky-blue linen scarf. Her red sandals displayed slim feet that seemed less tanned than he'd noticed earlier that day when she stood barefoot holding her flip-flops on the stone walk to the hotel.

'Am I late?' she asked, sensing he must have been seated for quite a while. He looked at her, smiled, and simply shook his head to mean *What could have made you think you were late?*

'I always worry.'

'Why, are you always late?'

'No, never, but I do worry all the same. My ex used to be the opposite.'

'How do you mean?'

'He used to come ahead of time, which always gave me the impression that I'd kept him waiting.' Then on thinking more, 'But why am I telling you this?'

'I don't know, why?'

Then, suddenly, with that same sly, quizzical look on her face she'd worn a few hours earlier, she couldn't resist asking, 'But you must have known this about me. Don't you know everything?'

'Oh, I see,' he said, as they brought the slices of raw fish he'd ordered a couple of hours earlier. The waiter meanwhile explained what sort of fish it was, when it was caught, and which olive oil the chef had used. The oil was a touch peppery, but nothing to intimidate anyone.

'Would you allow me to apologize once again?' he said, ignoring the waiter who was about to explain the garnish on the vegetable medley but decided to leave them alone.

'You don't have to.'

'But I want to.'

'Why?'

'I don't know why.'

At this they both laughed.

'Contrary to what you think, I don't know everything. Sometimes things just come to me and I am not always able to hold my tongue. But please tell me why I upset you so much.'

'I'm not sure I know either.'

'Was it the truth about your name or your birthday that you didn't want to hear or was it just my excavating private facts about Basil's twin that bothered you?'

'Maybe both, the fact is it scared me how you could be so totally right about things that no one knew a thing about and that those who did had totally forgotten. It frightened me, especially about

72

the cannibalized twin. Or maybe I didn't want to hear that at all.'

'So sorry.' He reached out and placed his right palm over her left hand. She did not remove it. But he removed his.

'This will be fantastic fish, I promise,' he said, changing the conversation.

'Do you know everything about fish as well?' she asked as she cut a slice. This, he figured, was a tacit little jab. But he liked it.

'Absolutely not. In fact, I know nothing about cooking.'

'You never cook for yourself?'

'Almost never.'

After the raw fish appetizer came another fish, this time grilled. They had a salad, then dessert, all accompanied by one of the best white wines of the region. At the end of their meal they were served a grappa.

It was nearing four when they decided to order a second round of grappa. After the tall septua-genarian waiter had finished pouring Raúl finally told her how happy he was that she had accepted his invitation to lunch.

'Moments like these happen so rarely in life. I just hope I'm not keeping you from your friends.'

'You're not keeping me from my friends,' she said, echoing his very words to suggest an implicit touch of humour. 'But then, you knew I was free this afternoon, didn't you?'

'I know facts, or the general contour of facts, not feelings or what goes on in someone's mind. Which is why I've not always been lucky in my life when it came to people. I'm not sure I've ever learnt how to read people.'

'You don't look like the sort who misreads people or who's been unlucky in life.'

He gave a heedless half-shrug, half-nod. 'I've been lucky in my life. True. But there again, lucky in facts, lucky with things, but not in what mattered most to me.'

She stopped drinking from her tiny grappa glass and held it in mid-air: 'Meaning love?'

'Exactly.'

'Has anyone really been lucky when it comes to love?'

'A few have. Not many. But I know some who have,' he said with doubt still lining his features, which meant he wasn't entirely convinced, which is why the two of them ended up laughing.

'Aren't you married?' she asked.

'I've been married. Once when I was in my thirties, and once eleven years ago. And there have been people in between, but now that I look back, I realize I've never loved any of the women I've lived with.'

'Not one?'

'Well, one, yes.'

'Was this recently?'

'No, when I was in my early twenties. The ones before her I don't remember at all and those who came after were just stopgaps, placeholders, fillers. When I look back . . .' But he didn't finish his sentence.

The silence that hung between them on that mild afternoon was not unpleasant. She threw her head back to better enjoy the weather and the late-afternoon light, or perhaps it was simply her body showing how pleased she was to be spending a quiet afternoon this way. When he looked down, he saw that she had removed her red sandals and was resting her feet on the warm gravel. He could hear her raking the pebbles with her toes, softly, slowly. When they had finished drinking, he asked if she would take a walk with him, not too far from the hotel grounds. She didn't say no. He put on his straw hat and, before stepping onto the dirt-paved road outside the hotel lobby, stood still for a moment. 'I love the sound,' he said.

'What sound?'

'The total silence. Turtle doves far, far away, the clamour of one or two kids playing in the bay, the occasional lawnmower droning quietly on a pleasant summer afternoon while everyone is still napping. I never nap.'

'I never nap either.'

'Yes, I know.'

She nodded.

'Have I been forgiven?' he asked.

She smiled at him. 'The jury is still out.' Then, thinking he might misread her: 'Clearly you have. See what a simple but wonderful lunch can accomplish?'

She slipped into her sandals and stood next to him.

'Come. We'll take a short walk.'

She thought he was going to take her along the shore, instead he led her outside the hotel grounds then up a hill that was covered with marine pines. It led to a narrow unpaved road that finally worked its way through what looked like a wood. The wood was unusually silent and gave off an air of intense peace and tranquillity she had seldom encountered before. She stopped and breathed in the scent of pines. 'Heavenly,' she said.

'Isn't it?' he added, and he too stopped to breathe in the light afternoon air. 'A few more yards and we're there,' he said.

When they reached the end of the wood they arrived at a flat plot of land, 'the field of melons', he said. The smell there was overpowering and enticingly sweet and stirred a bewildering sense of hunger, which the act of eating could never soothe, the way, he said, certain scented soaps stimulate a desire to bite into them, which everyone knows not to do.

Finally, they arrived at a garden that boasted exotic plants that had never been planted elsewhere in Europe. 'The son of the original owner of more than a century ago,' he explained, 'had sailed to the Far East and brought back seeds, which he secretly planted against his father's wishes. This is why the garden was hidden in the woods. He spent years planting these fruit trees in secret until his father's death. But by then the garden had blossomed and could no longer be moved. So, it stayed hidden here. Many of the plants perished, of course, but some survived and thrived.' Was she interested in plants and gardens? he asked.

'Not at all,' she replied. 'Or didn't you know?'

'I suspected,' he replied, smiling to signal he was aware of her insinuation. 'Still, I wanted to show you something.'

After pushing a gate that grated loudly against the ground before letting them inside, he turned around to let her take in a view of the other bay that she had never known existed. Under the spellbinding afternoon sun, it felt as though they were standing a mile above the sea.

'Is this what you wanted to show me?'

'No,' he replied. 'This here is the spice garden – of no interest to people who are not interested in gardening,' he added after bending down and rubbing his hand on a plant that stood knee-high. He then brought his palm to her nose: 'Smell this.'

'What is it?' she said, brusquely withdrawing her face from the reach of his palm.

'Smell it first.'

'Yes, but what is it?' she kept asking before consenting to smell it.

'You don't trust me, do you? Here, rub your hands on these leaves and smell.' She finally relented. She seemed surprised.

'I know this smell. Reminds me of something, but I can't tell what.'

'It's lovely, isn't it?' Then giving her time to reflect, he added: 'Almost like lemongrass, but not lemongrass, and like lavender, but not lavender. And yet I'll bet you've never smelt it before, though it stirs something like memory, but then, not memory. Shakes up your limbic system, though, doesn't it?'

'But I know it.' She leant down and tore a stem off the plant to take with her. 'I love this scent,' she said.

As they continued to walk through the muddy ground, they eventually came upon a small hut where a gardener sat on a stool, repairing a rake.

'*Commendatore*,' he said, rising to his feet.

Raúl greeted him and told him that he wanted to borrow the long pole to shake some fruit from the tree for the signorina.

'Does everyone know you here?' she asked.

'I spent all my summers here. None of those who grew up in this area have moved, and all have kept the same jobs. Time stops here. In fact, when I come here, I do nothing. I like doing nothing. You saw me working the hotel grounds. That's the most I do.'

The gardener went into the shed and came out with an old pole.

He offered it to Raúl but then said he would be perfectly willing to knock some of the fruit off for him. But Raúl said he'd do it himself, he'd been doing it since childhood.

'I wanted you to tell me what you thought. It's not a passion fruit, but it has a nuance of passion fruit and of pomegranate, maybe guava. But no one knew what to call it, so they called it *frutta dell'ira*, fruit of wrath, though no one knows why, possibly because the owner of the land hated that his son was planting so many exotic plants and trees here and kept scolding him. Or maybe because the fruit has growths like goosebumps and overgrown pimples and turns so red at this time of the year.'

As they approached the tree, she thought she saw something move. 'There are all manner of birds here, but they're very timid, and quiet. Follow me.'

When they finally reached a tall, lean tree, he pointed to what looked like full-blooded ruby spiky pears at the topmost reaches of the tree. 'Hence the pole,' he said. 'I used to rob this tree of so much fruit once.' And having said that, he started poking one of the fruits until it was finally freed from its twig and came tumbling down through stems and branches. He managed to catch it with both his hands.

He inserted both thumbs into it, opened it, and released a huge number of very tiny black seeds that looked like caviar or guava seeds. 'Sometimes they have tiny worms inside, but this one is totally clean. Want to try a taste?'

'*Frutta dell'ira?*' She questioned its name.

'*Frutta dell'ira.* My mother used to peel off the skin, remove all the seeds, then slice up the fruit and let the whole thing sit in lemon juice. It was naturally quite sweet, which is why she added salt. I have the most amazing memories of this fruit salad. But ever since she died, no one makes this dessert any longer.'

'Did you grow up here?'

'Only during summers. Our house is on the other side of the hill. I'll take you there sometime.'

'When?' The suddenness of her question surprised him. He looked at her and smiled.

'Tomorrow, if you like.'

'Are we having lunch too?'

'If you wish, of course.'

'Will you order the exact same thing?'

'Yes, easily. But don't you find me boring?'

'No.'

'Maybe slightly?'

'Well, yes, especially when you ask like this.' She tasted the fruit, pondered, finished her half of it while he bit into his half, all the while watching her.

'Pomegranate but not pomegranate. Maybe guava, but not guava.'

He looked at her, baffled. It took him a moment to realize she was teasing by echoing words he'd spoken moments earlier.

'Ever had this before? Bring back any memories?'

'Very, very vaguely. But I don't know of what. But it is sweet.'

He did not wait to be asked and, using the rod, released another fruit. But he did not let go of the rod in time so that the fruit came crashing down, splattering its contents on the ground.

'Pity.'

He tried for another. This time she caught it. She did what he had done and pressed it open, and breaking a twig from one of the trees, used it to scrape off the seeds.

She liked the fruit. 'The fruit salad shouldn't be too difficult to make. I wonder why they call it *frutta dell'ira*.'

'And I thought you weren't interested in plants or gardens.'

She told him she was a good cook.

'Yes, I know,' he said, then caught himself. 'Let's go back,' he added.

'So, lunch tomorrow then?' she asked.

'Same time, same spot,' he replied.

They returned the way they had come and parted at the entrance to the hotel, where her friends were waiting for a swim.

'Tomorrow, come with a bathing suit. I'll show you the Baia di Montesacro, a place no one knows exists.'

She waved goodbye, and had already taken off her sandals. 'And thank you for lunch.'

He shrugged his shoulders to mean no need for thanks, no fussy formalities, no pressure, it was, after all, entirely his pleasure.

CHAPTER FOUR

When he arrived, she was already seated at his table. He removed his sunglasses and was happy to notice that she had taken his seat, most likely to allow him to have the shade this time.

She was wearing a straw hat, the top of her bathing suit and a skirt. 'I did what you said.'

He was wearing shorts, a loose linen shirt and a cotton sweater with the sleeves wrapped around his neck and, like her, a straw hat. 'Still, a lovely surprise,' he said.

'I thought this was the plan.'

'Yes, I know, but I'm still very happy we're having lunch again.'

By then almost all the tables had been set for dinner and the patrons had left. 'I want to order the exact same things we ordered yesterday.'

They ordered the same white wine, the same raw fish salad, and as for the fish, it was indeed the same as the previous day's, except it was that day's catch.

'But we'll try a different dessert.'

'No *frutta dell'ira* ice cream?'

'If only!'

He liked that she remembered, liked that she didn't hide recalling its name.

'Enjoy the wine because on a day like today, it is the most amazing thing on planet Earth.'

'I agree.'

'After we're done, I'll show you a couple of spots tourists never see.'

The appetizers came. She ate her roll, then borrowed some of his, then simply took all of it. He enjoyed watching her eat. She noticed he was looking at her. Finally, she said, 'You're staring.'

'Yes, I am.'

She gave a faint, quiet smile, then continued cutting her fish. 'Why?'

'Because I like that we are friends.'

She gave a pensive nod. 'Me too.'

'Most people won't say this.'

'But I do.'

When they were done, and standing up, he watched her slip her feet easily back into the red sandals he had admired less than twenty-four hours earlier.

They walked along the *strada bianca*. Except for the few salespeople headed hastily to their gift shops, the road was totally empty under the intense afternoon sun. Margot had to stop a moment, complaining that a pebble had gotten into her sandal and was bothering her. He held her hand, as she removed her sandal, couldn't find the pebble, shook the sandal some more, then, leaning on his shoulder, put the sandal back on. He noticed that her sandal had left a slim x-shaped pattern of lighter skin on her otherwise tanned foot.

'Is it far?' she asked.

'Not at all.'

Within ten minutes they had reached the end of a road that led to the highway. 'Almost there,' he said. And sure enough, they stepped over an old, collapsed, weather-beaten wooden fence that opened the way to the shore and then they proceeded down the very slim arm of land that cut deep through the bay and then curved inward, almost creating a semicircle, which explained why not even a ripple reached the shore here. There was no sign of civilization, as though neither the Greeks nor the Romans nor the original inhabitants of the area had ever touched this spot of land where even the aged olive trees, which grow in phalanx formation elsewhere on the Italian peninsula, were scattered wildly about and seemed untended by human hands. As always, the tireless chorus of the cicadas and the moan of turtle doves. It was the most peaceful spot on earth and the sea, under the languorous mid-afternoon light, was as calm and limpid as a beautiful pair of sloe-eyes that never shed tears.

'Does anyone swim here?'

'People did once. But everyone prefers the crowded resort beaches. Want to try?'

She nodded.

'I still come here in the morning. No one, not a single soul, ever comes. And when you want shade, the ancient olive groves are happy to oblige. There are fig trees behind, and the figs are free for the taking come August through September.'

She wanted to walk along the shore and dip her toes in the water.

'This is my spot,' he said, and began removing his clothes down to his swimming suit.

She hesitated for an instant but he had turned his back and let her undress. She even removed her watch and her necklace and simply dumped them on her clothes. She still looked around nervously, as though still uncertain there really was no one, then raced towards the water.

By that hour of the day the sunlight had grown diffuse and the glare more muted, and once the two had crawled out till their feet could no longer touch bottom, they treaded water feeling a sense of plenitude and pure bliss wash over them. 'Look behind you,' he said, pointing to the shore. When she turned to look, the bay suddenly appeared so very distant and more deserted and more paradisiacal than she could have imagined.

'There's not a thing to want here,' he said.

'You're so right.'

'This, according to legend, is possibly where the lotus eaters lived.'

'You mean Ulysses' companions who refused to sail back to Ithaca? I can see why now,' she said, once again making light of her college education.

'I love walking all the way here, love reading here under the shade of one of those trees, and then love the walk back, with sand still in my sandals, which takes me back to my childhood when I used to hate having sand trapped in my sandals and preferred walking barefoot. Coming here reminds me that I do love planet Earth, that I like being alive, that I might even like myself.'

'Don't you always feel like this?'

'No,' he replied, almost too rapidly. 'I already told you. No one I know does. Some pretend to, others try hard to fool themselves, but no one likes who they truly are, except in spurts. When I feel

the sun on my skin and the water nearby and happen to like where I am, I try my best to coddle the
feeling. The only other things that come close for
me are chamber music and tennis.'

'And nothing else?'

'Sometimes that too. But not always.' They decided to crawl farther out. 'You swim well!' he said.

'Parents. Came with tennis and piano lessons.
You're a good swimmer yourself.'

'This was my beach once upon a time. I used to
come here with my mother, then I got in the habit
of coming alone, and then with someone special.'

'The one and only?'

'The one and only.'

'What would you pay me not to tell my friends
about this stretch of beach?'

'You won't tell them.'

'How do you know?' she asked, dunking under-
water then coming back up and throwing her hair
back while passing both palms along her face and
nose.

'Because this is our spot, yours now and mine,

and no one else's,' he replied, then looked away at the distant eastern arm of the bay.

'Proprietary, aren't we!' she said.

'Maybe. Yes.'

He asked if she could spot the very tip of the land extension before them. She said she could. He told her that there used to be a structure there once and asked if she had any idea what it might have been. They'd taken it down decades before.

She thought for a moment then said, 'I suppose a lighthouse. Most likely abandoned at least a century and a half ago.'

'Why abandoned?'

'Just a hunch. What would a lighthouse be doing here, anyway?'

He agreed with her. They both said it would have been a small lighthouse. 'Striped black and white, you think?' he hazarded.

She thought a while. 'No. I suspect it must have been more like a squat little hut made of stacked boulders with a strange round attic-looking structure from which scant light emanated to warn mariners of rocks and shoals. But I doubt it even gyrated as lighthouses do elsewhere.'

'When I was a boy,' he said, 'there used to be such a structure there, but totally abandoned in those days. My mother once told me that it was used by the Germans during the war. I was never allowed to go near there for fear of unexploded mines underfoot. But eventually, once you swam to the rock where we're headed, you could actually walk along the very shallow edge of land and reach the lighthouse.'

They continued to swim till they reached the large rock. 'As an adolescent I used to come here to be alone. Like being on another planet and stepping totally out of time. A wonderful feeling of pure quiet and pure being at one with the world.'

'I've never felt such wonderful water before,' she said. 'I even like its taste.'

'Welcome to the Tyrrhenian Sea.'

He climbed on the rock and sat on what was clearly his usual spot. Then he reached with his hands for hers and helped her climb up.

'Do you always bring women up here?'

'Never.'

'Except for the one and only?'

'The one and only, yes. But that's forty years and two months ago.'

'And how many days?'

'I can tell you if you need to know.'

She did not answer.

'We used to bring fruit and sit as we're doing now.'

'Dark grapes, I'm betting?'

'Yes, there's something about seawater and fruit. Then I realized what it was. Salt makes fruit sweeter.'

'Next time we'll remember to bring fruit. How about the *frutta dell'ira*?'

'That was her favourite. We spent hours sitting on this rock, just as we're doing now. And we spoke, spoke so much, and laughed even more than we spoke.' He stopped for a second. 'I'm happy you're here, though.'

'Though?' she immediately asked.

'I meant, I'm happy it's you here.'

She didn't know exactly what to add, or whether she'd understood his answer. She paused. 'I find myself . . . I find myself strangely envious of her, of the two of you, and I don't even know why.'

'We were so young at the time, so young. Nothing held us back.' He found himself deflecting the subject, as though something hovered between them, and neither wished to bring it up.

'From here we can swim to the very tip of the eastern arm of the bay.'

She nodded.

'Afterwards we'll either walk to where we left our clothes, or swim back. Then we'll dry on the sand. With this heat one dries in no time.'

They visited the spot where the lighthouse once stood and where the Germans had set up a make-shift post, then swam back to shore. They waited a short while then walked to the fallen fence and there, having dried themselves, put on their clothes.

He gave her his cotton sweater, which she slipped on over her head, tugging down the sleeves. She liked its smell. It surprised her. 'This was just lovely,' she said. 'I wonder what people will think seeing me arrive wearing your sweater.'

'They can think whatever they please.'

Without putting their sandals on but letting their feet drag through the sand to dry faster, they reached the end of the eastern arm of land that suddenly looked more like a jetty extending far off into the water and into sunlight.

As they continued walking he bent down and picked up a pumice stone, then offered it to her.

'I haven't seen a real wild pumice stone in my life. Thank you. Those they sell nowadays in the States have such tiny holes, they look and feel like pieces of cement cut small to fit your palm.'

She toyed with the stone and seemed fascinated by its lightness. 'Should we head back?' she asked.

'Soon. I'll take you by way of a shortcut. It's on the other side of the hill. Much prettier.'

The shortcut Raúl had in mind lay hidden off the coast and crossed the main street of the adjacent town. And indeed, as they approached, Margot saw that it was milling with tourists and vacationers stopping at one high-end shop after another, with the occasional gelato vendor, enoteca and espresso bar.

'Unbelievable, but this used to be a dirt-poor fishing hamlet once – now it's a beautified Potemkin village. Its stores used to sell fruits, vegetables, and always fish.'

Raúl stepped inside one of the bars, purchased two small bottles of sparkling water and handed Margot a bottle.

'How did you know I was dying for water?'

'Why didn't you say anything?'

'Actually, I didn't think of it.'

They stopped for a short while as they drank from their respective bottles.

'This is exactly like every tourist town on both Italian coastlines. One boutique after the other with the de-rigueur porcelain shop bearing regional patterns and motifs that are manufactured and painted elsewhere.'

'Were none of these stores here?'

'Not one.'

'What was this, a bus depot?'

'And what else?'

She looked around her and couldn't begin to know what this town had once been.

'Just take a guess,' he prodded.

'A garage? A movie theatre?' – and then she corrected herself – 'A slaughterhouse?'

'What made you guess a slaughterhouse?' he asked.

'No idea.' She looked around and saw a plaque that read *Piazza del Macello*. 'Maybe because I read the plaque without realizing it.'

'Do you even know what *macello* means in Italian?'

'No.'

'Then how could it have helped you guess what used to be here?'

'I don't know. Why are you cross-examining me?!'

'Am I upsetting you?'

'A little, yes.'

'Why?'

'I don't know why, but you are.'

He explained that he simply wanted to show her how this rinky-dink little place had become, from nothing, a hotbed of high-end shops. 'Take a look at this triple cinema, playing the same superhero film in all three theatres. In my day there was no cinema here.'

'What was there?' She looked at the theatres, trying to visualize what he was remembering.

'Any child could tell you that.'

'What, a bus depot for some of those tiny buses running up and down the coast?'

'And near the depot?'

'How would I know. A winery? You're quizzing me again.'

'No, I'm not.'

'Yes, you are.'

'Okay, so I was a bit. This whole new building, which is made to look Gothic, was something else in my day. It was a huge, helter-skelter, improvised amusement park that lasted only a few weeks. My parents used to take me there. Then, the poles and tents and swing carousels and bumper cars would suddenly disappear until the following year.'

So saying they walked up a narrow road neatly paved with cobblestones that were embedded into the ground in arched patterns. When they reached the top of the hill, they found a lovely tea hut with crowded tables and chairs where those who had come for shopping were taking a rest. Beyond the teahouse they spotted a large rectangular nineteenth-century villa surrounded by rich vegetation and a flower garden, next to which stood a similar house, but much smaller, built to seem like its younger sister. Both houses had mansard roofs and looked nothing like any building in southern Italy.

'Feels like Normandy,' she said.

'Not surprising. The man who had it built was a Frenchman who wanted a French home overlooking the Tyrrhenian Sea. By the way, it leads directly down the hill to the beach where we swam. Come, I'll take you there.'

'You've been there before?'

'More times than I remember. This used to be our summer home. The smaller house was a guesthouse and a haven when we were kids, since this was where all the children of my parents' friends stayed.'

They walked up the hill and rang the bell. There was the sound of children playing inside.

Eventually they heard steps and a lady opened the door. She immediately exclaimed Raúl's name and hugged him very affectionately. They bandied their usual jokes: *You never come! You know I can't stand you. But we love you. Plus, your food is horrible.* Turning to Margot, Raúl informed her that Doriana was a cordon bleu chef. Introductions were made, Doriana insisted on serving tea. Margot said it wasn't necessary. Doriana persisted, Margot relented.

'You're worse than he is,' Doriana said, as Margot and Raúl entered the house. 'And I thought no one could be worse.'

'I wanted to show her the house. We'll stay for your horrible tea and cookies.'

And with that Doriana hopped into the kitchen, screaming at the children who massed around her when they heard the English word *cookie*.

'Next autumn they're all going back to boarding school, and I'll be done with the lot of them and finally have time to finish my book on the terrible end of Masaniello.' Then turning to Margot, 'I'm just a historian.'

'Come, I'll show you around,' said Raúl.

He walked her through the hallway then into the dining room, which led to a large terrace from which, once he opened the large French windows, one could watch the sea. It was a spellbinding, expansive view of the very late-afternoon blue. Raúl and Margot caught a view of the shore as well as the rock where they had lounged for a while, with a clear sight of the strip of land extending out into the sea like a ballerina's gesture of worship and insouciance.

He closed the windows and walked her to the living room.

'I could have sworn there was a piano here,' she said.

'Here?' he asked.

'No, over there.'

'I don't know. Could have been. Maybe they moved it.'

'Yes, because where else would they have put the dark baroque bench with the carved lion head on each armrest?'

'What armrests with what lions' heads? I should know, I grew up in this house.'

'I was just imagining it,' she said.

He took her to the library. The books hadn't moved in more than a century. 'See that love seat over there?' He pointed at it. 'I used to read there. My little universe: Stendhal, Forster, Hardy and my favourites, Thucydides, Herodotus and Xenophon.'

'A love seat all to yourself!'

'This room was my kingdom. It hasn't changed one bit. Not the love seat, not the vases and ugly marble statuettes, not the memories always cluttering in. Let me take you upstairs.'

On the stairway up, however, she suddenly stood still, turned around and, looking out of the bay windows in the library, simply said: 'I know I've been here before.'

He did not say anything, but stared at the afternoon glow upon the stairs and to himself muttered, 'I know.'

CHAPTER FIVE

Doriana called them downstairs for tea on the veranda.

'This is such a beautiful house,' said Margot.

Doriana looked at her and smiled. 'It took forever for him to decide to let us live in it,' she said, pointing at Raúl. 'We changed so very little, except for the children's rooms. Even the china hasn't changed, cracked and chipped as everything is in this house. But then we like it that way.'

'Look at this dish,' she added, 'pure Limoges, but defaced thanks to the dishwasher, which we were told would scrape all the colours away and blandify everything. But did we listen?'

'The way you cook would scrape off the lining of every human stomach.'

'He never comes, no matter how many times I invite him.'

'And with good reason,' he retorted.

Margot took her cup and held it in both hands, then removed her red sandals and tucked both her feet on the bar under Raúl's wicker chair. 'This is heaven,' she finally said.

'You are welcome to come here anytime – not him, though!'

'Don't trust her. She'll cook dinner for you and the next thing is you won't tolerate anyone else's cooking, including your own. She's a Circe in the kitchen. After her chicken Marengo, you'll never be able to eat anyone else's chicken. To say nothing of her tarte Tatin! Ruins you for life.'

A moment of silence followed as all three sipped their tea and watched the setting sun cast glowing colours on the horizon.

'It's so peaceful here,' said Margot. 'The strange thing is that this is all too familiar, as if I've been on this very patio before.'

'Well, the house was designed by a French architect who built so many houses on the same model that it wouldn't surprise me if you've been in others as well. You'll find his houses in Poland and Hungary.'

'No, I've been here, in this house, on this very patio.'

Margot swore that there was a piano downstairs and a wooden love seat with sunken cushions and two armrests bearing the carved features of two lion heads. 'Plus, I'm almost sure I've been in the library, and especially up and down the stairway in the afternoon. And yet, I know this is my very first time here. I've never even been to the south of Italy before.'

'A déjà vu!' exclaimed Doriana, chewing on a biscuit.

Margot smiled back, but suddenly stiffened. She removed her feet from under Raúl's chair, put down her cup on the forged iron table with pointed metal leaves, looked around her and, turning to Raúl, said: 'If I believed in spells, I'd say I was under one. Am I under a spell?'

'Do people still believe in spells?' asked Doriana. 'You remind me of my grandmother.'

'Then what is happening? I can even recognize the patterns on the china now, faded or not,' said Margot.

'But everyone owns this kind of china the world over, you'll find it in any shop.'

Margot picked up her teacup again, but then put it back down on the table.

'I know where the bathroom is. And I know this house. I even know where an old sewing machine used to be.' And turning to Raúl, said: 'Explain.' And seeing he hesitated, 'Now!'

This was the moment he had feared the most. Leading up to it had been fun, even sweet, but this now was pure agony.

'Let's start with the lighthouse,' he said, 'then move on to the bus depot, then the slaughterhouse, finally the amusement park. We'll even throw in *frutta dell'ira.*'

'Yes, and?'

'You were amazingly right each and every single time. You were even right about the rock when we sat on it.'

'What did I say?'

'You spoke about grapes.'

'What about the grapes?' There were signs of vexation on her face.

'Would you let me explain?'

'Yes, go ahead, explain. Right now!'

'Just let me proceed at my own pace,' he said, giving her a chilling, momentary glance.

He stood up, went to a bookcase, and took down a large picture book of old black-and-white photographs taken by Luigi Alberti. 'Every family in the area owns this book,' he said, 'because it captures the landscape as it was immediately after the war.' He opened the book to the little town they had just visited. Here was the bus depot, there the amusement park, there the slaughterhouse, and just in case she had any doubts, on the cover of the book was a faded sepia picture of the long arm of the bay with a tiny square shed at its very tip – 'Just as you described it,' he said, 'the lighthouse.'

'But let me give you some background.' And so, he began to tell her about a young man whose family summered every year in southern Italy. The young man's uncle, who lived in England, had a twenty-two-year-old daughter. He and his wife were involved in such bitter divorce proceedings that they asked if the family might house their daughter in Italy for a few months before she was to return to Oxford later that autumn. She couldn't have been happier than to be spared the daily riot in her parents' home, where quarrels, insults and objects thrown around the dining room made her life intolerable.

But the student, as everyone would find out in less than a few days after she'd settled in their home late that spring, was hardly more tolerable than her parents. She was uncommonly impatient and harsh with the help in the house, and her speech and behaviour downright offensive with everyone, including her uncle, her mother's brother, who took her blunt manner in his stride and put up with her insolence whenever she criticized or mocked their home. She had taken up the bad habit of practising her violin in their living room for hours on end, which made family life impossible past mid-morning. Her morning snack was always left half-finished in the living room, and her coffee mug left round stains on one of the wooden cabinets.

But worst of all was her attitude towards the young man in the household. She contradicted and argued with everything he said and made no effort to hide her contempt for him. One evening, just a few days after she had moved in, she watched him walk into the living room to bid his parents good-night. He was on his way to a dinner party and was wearing a new suit. She looked him over, smirked, and said it was clear the suit was purchased off a rack somewhere. His tie didn't agree with his shirt, the shirt was too bright, the sleeves too long, and the jacket too wide. Had he, perhaps, purchased it expecting to put on weight in the years to come?

He was humiliated.

'These are no better,' she said after he'd rushed upstairs and taken off the suit, shirt and tie she'd derided and put on other clothes.

He began to dislike her even more. What particularly galled him was the way she was so visibly enamoured of herself. Every time she passed by a mirror or a dark glass panel, she could not resist casting a lingering look at herself, always checking her shirt, her hair, her face. Sometimes, when she spoke with someone, it was clear her eyes were focusing, not on the person to whom she was speaking, but on her face in the mirror.

For her part, she couldn't stand his snobbish airs each time he attempted to play master of the house when his father wasn't present. It was clear to everyone that, once he'd passed his law exams, he'd manage his father's affairs and eventually inherit his business. It was also very clear that he resented her presence and wanted her and her violin gone long before she was due back to either one of her beleaguered parents.

That summer he was cramming for the bar and the last thing he needed was an intruder upsetting his quiet home rituals with the perpetual droning of her instrument in their living room. Worse yet was her horrible habit of humming with her violin, sometimes literally singing along with the instrument. His mother tried a few times to speak to her about the sound and recommended she practise in another room, far from where her son was studying.

So here he was studying for the bar and there she was singing along, almost as though doing it on purpose. So finally, one day, he decided to take matters into his own hands and asked her to stop practising while he was studying. She asked if he would stop studying while she practised. Well, he had an exam, he said. And so did she, she replied. Then she should practise in her own home, not in his. They had a loud row at which he blew up and told her that she was not his sister and that this was not her home. 'Besides, you're not even your parents' daughter,' he added with a heavy note of sarcasm.

'Meaning what?' she said with derision tearing out of her voice.

'Meaning exactly what I've just said.'

She seemed puzzled.

'So, you didn't know, did you?' he finally asked.

'Didn't know what?'

He was not the type to mince words and told her that she and her parents didn't have a speck of blood in common; that her parents, who were second cousins, had more in common with each other than with her.

'You, dear girl,' he said, 'were adopted. No one knows who brought you into this world, so you are what is generally referred to as a mongrel.'

This shut her up. She was certain that he had made the whole thing up to hurt her, but as happens with unexpected revelations that suddenly seem to put everything in its place, his words had come with the ring of truth and, what was more surprising yet, didn't seem to upset her – as though she had always suspected but hadn't had the time or the means or the will to consider the matter further. But what surprised her even more than the revelation itself was the feeling of total relief that accompanied what she'd just heard, as if she had finally found a good reason to be rid of parents she'd wished to shun since childhood.

She had always had a strange hunch that she never belonged to them, but where that hunch was born, she had no idea. Still, this did not mean that she was going to accept the news from him. She yelled the loudest 'Liar!' anyone had ever screamed in his placid household and after slapping him in the face asked him to give her one iota of proof.

'You don't need proof. Your rage is proof enough,' he replied. No woman had ever slapped him before. It spoke of her sudden helplessness, and he liked having driven her to it. Seeing him smile after the slap sent her spiralling into a fit and she was about to scratch him on the face except that he grabbed both her wrists and asked if it wasn't time for her to start practising her fiddle now.

'You monster, you shithead.' Then she got a hold of herself. 'This news, for your information, is nothing new. The only difference now is that you're the shithead who's dotted the i's for me. Now leave the room.'

'No, you leave.'

She walked straight away out of the living room, muttering, 'You beast!' This is what she'd heard her mother exclaim to her father, neither of whom, as she'd just found out, was either her mother or father. 'And good riddance to the whole lot of you,' she yelped. She slammed the door shut behind her.

But later that day, thinking back on what he had told her, he realized he had gone too far. He knew now that she had every reason to hate him. He could already tell she hated everything about him, from the way she grimaced when he read verses out loud to his mother or the way she sighed each time he rubbed his hands with sunblock, just his hands, before heading out to the beach. He could see it in her eyes or when she grunted when he thought he was saying something profound while watching the news. Plus, he had his set habits and always needed to be the first to read the paper when it arrived in the morning. Everyone else in the family read it when they had a moment, sometimes long after lunch, or later in the evening. He was stuffy and fussy, and he seemed to know it and liked being that way, which is why she cut him down on the evening he had put on a suit before heading out to dinner with friends. She hated the way he rattled the car keys, hated the sound of his shoes when they hit the parquet floor, hated his laugh even. She even hated his horrible habit of pruning the skin off every mandarin segment, off every orange, or grapefruit, because he didn't like the skin of fruit, and would leave their naked sloughs drying on his plate like the shed skin of baby reptiles. He even wanted his tomatoes peeled, ditto with potatoes and cucumbers. There was not a thing she liked about him. Now she wanted him dead. And he could read it on her features. It amused him, as if he wanted her to hate him, because he too enjoyed hating her.

When his father asked him to apologize to her for something he had said, he refused, saying he'd never apologize to someone like her. He'd said this because he had heard his father ask her to apologize to him for something she too had said, which might have hurt his feelings. Her blunt reply was unforgettable: *I don't know how to apologize.*

Yet, despite their recent rows – and there were many – both were discreet enough not to let on to his parents how much they scorned each other or that he had told her the truth about her adoptive parents. At dinner the two of them were well behaved: 'Could you pass me the salt?' 'Of course. Here it is.' This the day after she had called him a beast. At breakfast, when they were seldom alone, they greeted each other with a seemingly hearty 'Good morning,' and when watching TV with the family on the evenings when neither was out, they always shared the same sofa. When they crossed each other either on the way in or out of the house or in the empty corridor, he would whisper 'Asshole,' and she would whisper back 'Shithead.' Once, on the stairs, and without meaning to, he accidentally elbowed her rather hard, while she right away kicked his shin with the edge of her sneakers. He yelled in pain. 'Teaches you,' she said. Then when she happened to trip against a breeze block in the garden, he couldn't help exclaiming, 'Hope it hurts.'

But when he saw her bleeding from her wrist after she had cut herself against the slightly protruding, large, pointed leaf of a forged-iron table in the garden, he rushed to fetch a spool of gauze from one of the medicine cabinets and applied rubbing alcohol generously on the cut before wrapping the gauze tightly three times around her wrist. He couldn't decide which had given him more pleasure as he helped staunch the bleeding: proving useful in a moment of need and showing his expertise in treating a wound or watching her reaction once the alcohol burnt her. 'You did it on purpose,' she said, referring to the alcohol. He smiled, all the while applying pressure to the cut with his thumb as he tied the knot around it.

'I did,' he said.

'There's no need for so much alcohol.'

'At least you won't need stitches.'

'I'm not an idiot,' meaning any idiot could tell that stitches weren't needed.

'Well, you are an idiot,' he said, and left her in the garden with the bottle of alcohol and roll of gauze for her to return them to the medicine cabinet.

'Right,' she replied. 'Don't let me hold you up.'

But he was already gone and out of earshot.

Later that same afternoon when she was lying on the beach, he passed by with a glass bottle of cold water. 'Can I have a sip of water?' he heard her say. 'I forgot to bring my own.' Without thinking he threw the bottle on the sand next to her. She was not unaware of his contemptuous gesture, but was thirsty enough not to show any sign of anger or say anything about his manner. She simply brushed the sand off the bottle, removed the cap, and took a few sips. Then seeing that some sand had landed on her towel as well, she brushed it away, then raising her eyes, looked at him and made a gesture to give him back his bottle. 'Why do you hate me?' she suddenly asked.

He did not have time to think of an answer and simply tossed out the first one that came into his mind. 'I don't know.'

'But you must have some idea.'

He shrugged his shoulders. 'Do you know why you hate me?'

She shook her head, meaning she didn't know and didn't care to know either. 'We're even then.'

'I guess.'

She asked him if it was normal for the wound on her wrist to throb.

'Yes and no,' he replied, and said he'd need to take another look. She simply raised her wrist to allow him to inspect it.

He cautiously unwrapped the bandage he had made hours earlier, compared her right wrist to her left, said it wasn't swollen or red, and, cupping her wrist in one palm, asked if this hurt a bit. 'You did it on purpose,' she said after he had pressed the wound a tiny bit. He did not allow himself to answer her accusation but recommended she use the antibacterial ointment to be found in the medicine cabinet in the guest bathroom. He let go of her wrist, stood up, and was all set to walk away.

'Didn't you want your bottle back?' she asked.

'Keep it.' He said these words with the habitual dismissive inflection he used whenever speaking to her.

'You didn't have to hurt me, you know.'

'I didn't mean to,' he replied.

'Why don't I trust a thing you say?'

'I may be a complete shithead,' smirking as he used her word, 'but I'm not a psycho.'

She looked at him and said nothing, but it was clear she was mulling a sharp and cruel rebuke to his perfunctory apology.

'You don't think this could lead to sepsis, do you?' she finally asked.

'I've seen worse cuts.'

He offered to get her the ointment.

'Don't bother,' she said.

'Suit yourself.'

And with this he walked away.

The next morning at breakfast, 'How is it?' he asked.

'Better.'

And this was all they said. He read the paper, she reviewed the Bach Chaconne, he spoke to his mother, she spoke to her uncle.

On the beach, when she was lying on her stomach with her bikini top off, he came up to her and, kneeling down, asked to see the cut.

'No need,' she snapped.

He stood up again. 'I was just offering.'

'I can tell it's doing better,' she replied, sensing that perhaps she had been overly brusque with him. 'But take a look if you have to.'

'I promise I won't touch the cut.'

'And here I was looking forward to having the wound pinched, maybe even squeezed.'

'I told you I wasn't a pervert.'

'No, you said something else.'

'I was only echoing your word.'

It made the two of them laugh.

'You know,' she said, 'we really have no reason to hate each other. I'm not a bad person, and I'm sure you aren't either.'

He decided not to argue.

'Would you do me a huge favour? Though it might totally deplete today's ration of superficial good will.'

'What?'

'I can't use my wrist. Could you put some sunblock on my left shoulder?'

He grabbed her tube of sunblock and began rubbing her right shoulder with it.

'Wrong shoulder,' she said.

'I know. I want to cover both, so you don't look ridiculous with an uneven tan. I know how important your looks are to you.'

But as he was spreading the suntan lotion on her shoulders, and then on her back, he found he didn't mind touching her skin. The more he applied the cream, the slower and more lingering his hand movements.

'What are you doing?' she finally asked, sensing something different in his touch.

'Just spreading the sunblock,' he replied. But then he asked her to raise herself just a tad and, without hesitating, began to apply the cream on her left breast, then her right breast. 'So, they don't get sunburnt,' he said, smiling.

She did not say anything, and simply followed with her eyes the slow tempered motions of his palm as it caressed and kept caressing her breasts. Then, looking around at his bathing suit and sounding totally surprised, she simply said: 'Oh, I see.'

He did not say anything, but kept caressing one shoulder, then the other, back to the first, then to her breasts long after the cream had been spread and was fast drying on his hands. Then he reached for her tube and began applying more cream to his hands and then to the back of her neck, and to her bare back and the back of her arms.

'What are you doing to me?' she asked again.

This time, he did not reply.

'What are you doing to me!' he finally said.

Again she looked.

Which is when she suddenly managed to lift herself, put back her bikini top as best she could with one hand, and roll up the towel she had brought with her from the house. She stood and, leaning down with her knees almost touching his chin, picked up her sunglasses, her magazines, the tube of sunblock from his hand, and headed home.

But her words *What are you doing to me?* wouldn't let go of him and resonated in his mind all morning as he lay stunned on the deserted beach. He suspected she was upset with him, but he also knew that, behind the veil of reproof in her words, meaning *How dare you do this to me?* her voice could have cradled an inflection of desire, astonishment, possibly surrender.

What are you doing to me?

No woman had said this to him before and the strain in her voice when she'd spoken these words cast a spell that wouldn't let go of him as he lay there unable to think or read or even focus on the quiet July waves rippling to the shore. He could think of nothing but the breasts of this woman he hated. Then, almost suddenly, he realized what her words had also stirred in him, for they were neither docile nor vulnerable nor moved by anger or even passion – they were savage. She was savage – not angry, not passionate. The way she had rolled up her towel and decided to put on the bikini top despite her wrist, and exposed herself in the process without embarrassment, the way she had snubbed him after looking and smirked was sudden, shameless, and, yes, savage.

Many hours later, when it was time for dinner, he ran into her on her way downstairs to the dining room.

Were they really going to push each other again as they'd done a few days earlier? She made a motion to let him pass by flattening her body against the curved wall of the staircase in a gesture that showed she was determined to avoid another shoving bout, even though both sensed that shoving after what had happened between them on the shore belonged to the past. But then he had done the exact same thing: by thrusting his body against the banister to let her pass, he too was suggesting that insults between them, let alone their habitual elbowing, were no longer something either wished to pursue. He read her exaggerated move to the wall as yet another instance of her overly theatrical nature, since he knew she was entirely driven by external gestures. Her reading of his own move against the banister was far more accurate. He is nervous, she thought, he likes me.

'Why did you touch me at the beach?' she asked as they proceeded down the stairs. She was expecting an answer.

Instead she got a question: 'Why did you let me?'

This did not please her, and he could tell she was about to turn mean again.

'Are we always going to be enemies?' he asked, hoping to stem the tempest before it erupted.

He had rehearsed that question and thought it was as good a way as any to bring back what had happened between them at the beach that morning.

'Are we enemies?'

With that she rushed downstairs to dinner. His heart was pounding. She's lying. She couldn't possibly mean what she'd just said.

Just before walking into the dining room where a guest and his wife were present, he found a moment to tell her that he couldn't believe a word of what she'd just said to him.

She smiled. 'I know.'

He couldn't help himself. 'You know that I shouldn't believe you or do you know that I don't?'

She looked at him again the way she'd just done and repeated: 'I told you, I know.'

No one in his life had puzzled him so. Everyone else he'd met was transparent, even when they tried to remain elusive.

'Do I scare you this much that you need to speak to me in riddles?'

She thought for a moment before greeting one of the guests.

'It's not you I'm scared of.'

'Of whom then?'

'*Of whom then*,' she mimicked. 'It's me I'm scared of. Me. You understand?'

He was totally baffled.

'Now you know.'

Not a word between them throughout the dinner. After dinner, she managed to catch him on his way upstairs.

'I'll come to your room.'

'When?' he asked.

'I don't know.'

That night he could not sleep. Each time anything in the house creaked, he was sure that she was opening his door. But then he realized that she was not the furtive type to go about the house on tiptoes, to open doors softly. Besides, he had left his door ajar, something he'd never done before, precisely to let her know she was welcome in. Why hadn't she come, then? Perhaps she had made her promise on the fly and had just meant to tease him with never a thought of going through with it. Or perhaps something he had said right after dinner had made her change her mind. Or had she simply fallen asleep and forgotten?

Sensing she wasn't coming, he resolved to make himself dream of her, and perhaps he did dream, though it wasn't exactly a dream, but just like a dream, during which all he did was revisit time and time again what she meant at the beach when she'd said *What are you doing?* and moments later, once he'd rubbed her breasts and begun to massage her feet, the heel, the arch, and then the toes and in between the toes of each foot, he'd heard *What are you doing to me?* And in his dream, all he replied was *You know exactly what I'm doing, of course you know, you've always known.* And then came the moment he savoured most but kept postponing each time he saw it coming from the periphery of his dreaming mind and enjoyed deferring as much as he could so as to arrive at it after many delays – the moment which he knew had happened when she had suddenly turned before standing up to leave the beach. Oh, she'd seen alright, and he liked that she'd seen, how couldn't she have, because this too was true about the two of them: they cared for each other so little as to harbour no shame, no qualms, nothing to hold them back, which is why he had touched her and why she'd let him, and why she'd seen and he was pleased that she had.

'You never came last night,' he said to her the next morning.

'Did I say I would?'

'I just wish you had.'

'I never apologize.'

He refused to speak to her. When he went to the beach later that day, he made a point of lying far away from her.

But then one morning, after he'd resolved never to give her another thought, he woke up and found her sitting on his desk chair staring at him.

'How long have you been there?'

'A while.'

'Just staring at me sleeping?'

'Yes.'

'Why?'

'Because I can learn so much about someone by watching him sleep.'

'What did you learn?'

'I learnt that you can be a very sweet man, but your sleep is not happy. You clench your jaws and you look angry sometimes, as though fighting demons.'

'Maybe I was thinking of you then.'

Realizing what he'd just said, he felt he needed to say more: 'All I do is think of you. I go to sleep thinking of you, dream of you, and wake up with this.' He wanted to shock her. She wasn't shocked.

'Seriously?' she said.

'And then one day I open my eyes and I find you in my bedroom.' He moved to the side of his bed and lifted the sheet again, clearly inviting her to his bed.

'No,' she said.

She did not know why she'd said *no* so gruffly, but she also enjoyed turning him down.

'You don't trust me?'

'I already told you. It's not you I don't trust.' And having said this, she left his room.

But a few nights later, he didn't have long to think before deciding to slip into her bedroom. Not knowing what to wear, he decided to put on his bathing suit. Her clothes were lying on a chair, so he plopped himself on the low wooden cabinet that housed the family's sewing machine and simply sat on it and watched her sleep even though it was getting colder by dawn.

'What are you doing?' she said when she finally opened her eyes.

'It's my turn,' he said.

She did not say anything, just looked at him and at his bathing suit. 'Were you planning to swim in my bedroom?'

They both laughed.

'I haven't decided. But I'm cold and this swimming suit at this hour is utterly ridiculous. I didn't know what to wear.'

'Aren't you cold?'

'Freezing.'

Using her feet, she pushed her sheet away and exposed her naked body. 'I've been thinking of you.'

She didn't have to add another word. He removed his bathing suit and, shivering, crawled into her bed. She hugged him, kept him warm with the weight of her body, and placing the palm of her hands on each side of his face said, 'I'm so glad you came.'

From that moment on, as if under a spell, the two were as inseparable as Tristan and Iseult.

What neither realized was that all their bile and venom and their contempt for each other was precisely what allowed instant intimacy to spread between them without their sensing, much less suspecting, that it had already happened. It didn't flourish, it didn't blossom, it simply sprang on them that day on the beach when he'd thrown his water bottle next to her on the sand and then touched her skin. Because neither even thought, much less wished there could be anything between them, they let their bodies decide, not their hearts, not their minds, not even the thrill of secrecy from everyone in the household. For all they knew, their one night together was going to happen once, and once only. But it was because they expected nothing, not even pleasure, that they couldn't let go of each other. This, as she, the Bach student, explained one day, was intimacy by *contrario motu*. They backed into each other's life and spent the remainder of that summer making love every moment they could. They never asked why they made love, but they made love without holding back, because, at least at first, they didn't seem to care what the other thought, or felt, or needed. What cleared their way was not friendship; it was enmity that fooled them.

They lasted four months, until October. She wanted to give up Oxford, he wanted to follow her there. They were smart enough to know that nothing lasts, least of all fiery passion – but they lay naked every morning on their rock, they made love every afternoon and every night, and sometimes they'd end up at the movies, interested in nothing and no one except each other. There wasn't a thing they didn't do together. She once asked him if this was real. 'Does any of it not feel real?' he'd answered. 'No.' 'So why ask?' 'Because we need to ask, because we need to know, because I fear the worst.' 'If you're going to England, I want to be on the same plane with you. If you're ever on a boat, I want to sail on it. If you're crossing the street even, I'll walk with you.'

She died in a car accident not five miles away. She had just turned twenty-two. There was bad light that night, the twisting roads along the cliff were slippery, and the fog dense. He should have stopped her. Something told him, though, the moment he remembered that they had never once, not once, used the word love. That's how he suddenly knew that something was amiss. The thought wouldn't have come to him otherwise. But he didn't trust himself and chose to overlook the signs.

'I can do many things,' Raúl said, 'I can cure someone's back pain, let kidney stones dissolve into nothing, make tempests happen, stop boats from sailing. When I was a boy, I could make the school bus arrive late at school, have parking spaces suddenly materialize so my father wouldn't get upset, even have the food ready long before we stepped into a restaurant or had even ordered. But this was beyond me.'

He was quiet for a moment.

'"One day," I told her, "we could lose interest in whatever we have and be back to hating each other – ramming each other up and down the stairwell." "But then," she said, "I'll hurt myself and you'll tend to my cut and before we know it, you'll slip into my bedroom wearing that swimming suit, asking to be kept warm, and we'll swim out to our rock and make love there till dawn catches us freezing."'

'Do I remind you of her? Were you thinking of making love to me when we were on the rock together?' Margot asked.

'You don't understand.'

'What don't I understand?'

'I did make love to you on the rock. Except . . .'

'Except?'

'Except it was forty years ago. Her name, as I'm sure you've guessed by now, was Marya. But looking back now, it was I who died, not she, I who've been dead my whole life, except . . .'

'Except, again?'

'Except she is you, and you are more alive today than I've ever been.'

Margot heard him say this and bristled. It made her entire life feel like a fraud, as though her life as Marya, if indeed it was a previous life, took precedence over everything she'd lived, known and done. She wasn't prepared to accept this shadow-self, she said.

'Please don't be angry with me. It was not my intention to belittle your current life, or to ask the previous one to compete with it, or take it over. All I wanted was to be with you – for a few hours, for a few days, that's all.' He paused.

'Before we leave this house, which you may never want to see again, at least not with me and certainly not when I'm alive, I want to show you something,' he said.

'What?' she asked. By now she'd grown restless and hostile.

He did not tell her what. Instead, he led her up the stairs to the first floor – 'This is the famous stairway,' he said, knowing she'd understand – and then up to the second floor. He opened the door to a small room.

'I know the smell of that room,' she said. 'I know that smell.'

'It was once your room. You do know what stood here, on this very spot.' He could tell that she had already guessed, or rather, had always known. She did not have to say.

'Correct,' he replied. 'And I want you to see this,' he said, opening a closet. 'We saved it as a keepsake. But I kept it, knowing you'd be back to see it one day.' He took it out of its case, then unwrapped its felt covering.

'May I?' she asked, meaning to touch it.

'It's yours. You can take it now, if you wish.'

'Seriously?' she asked as she rubbed a palm delicately on its glistening maple back.

'Very seriously.'

'But I've never played.'

He smiled.

'But why are you giving it to me?'

'It's the only proof I have that you are who you are, that you are back. You see, you didn't die, you just went away.'

'I can't take it.'

'Well, think about it. Promise? It's yours.'

She nodded.

'I also want to show you something else,' he said.

'What now?'

He ignored her tone and opened the other cupboard door, which revealed a linen closet. He put his hand under a thin sheet of cloth lining one of the tiny shelves filled with folded tablecloths and coloured napkins and pulled out a square envelope from underneath. He opened the unsealed envelope and produced a coloured snapshot of a young man and a young woman wearing bathing suits. They're both smiling broadly and squinting a bit, probably because of the sun in their face. In the distance lies the rock. She is holding a plastic bag while attempting to hide it behind her back. Her hair is short, the two of them are very tanned.

'Marya?' Margot asked.

'Marya,' he replied.

'She looks like me.'

'She is you.'

'We even have the same knees, and the same feet.'

'Same elbows,' he added, as she raised her elbows to take a better look at them.

She agreed.

'The two of you look so alike,' she said.

'I know. Sometimes we felt we were the same person.'

'So, you've kept this photo.'

'Of course I've kept it. It's the only picture I have of the two of us.'

'Who took the picture?'

'Someone.'

'What's in the plastic bag that she's trying to hide from the picture?'

'You know the answer. Fruit. She'd just rinsed it in seawater.'

Again Margot stared at the picture.

'Take it,' said Raúl.

'I can't take it. It's yours.'

'It means more to me now if you take it. Plus . . .'

'I hate when you do this. Plus what?'

'There's a reason why I want you to have it.' He waited a few seconds. 'I want you to remember the face of the young man in the picture.'

'Why?'

'You'll meet him when you're my age.'

'You make the rest of my life feel so joyless, so totally pointless.' She gave what she'd just said some thought. 'Just take me back to our hotel.'

Together they left the room and walked down the old stairwell.

CHAPTER SIX

On their way, she walked much faster than they'd done earlier, either in a rush to get back to the hotel or determined now to show that she was keeping her distance. He was not surprised. She had to shower and change, she said. Her friends were planning a night out at one of the clubs in the hills. He bid her good evening and they separated in the lobby as she entered the elevator – but then suddenly she stepped out again. All manner of hopes raced through his mind when he saw her exit so swiftly and was sure he had totally misjudged her. With a simple gesture, she removed her sweater and gave it back to him before rushing back into the elevator.

Later, when he walked into the dining area to his usual table by the illuminated pool, her friends hailed him.

'Malcolm was asking if you had any more tips for him,' said Basil.

'All out of tips tonight. Send him my apologies.'

Oscar showed him his new hat. 'My newest conquest.'

Raúl congratulated him. 'And the shoulder?' he asked Mark.

'Couldn't be better.'

She did not greet him, but continued to chat with Angelica; nor did she even turn to look at him, though he knew she was aware of his presence at the table where barely a few hours earlier he'd had one of his happiest lunches in so many years. *Strange*, he thought, she didn't use to be so chatty with everyone and now she was all ebullient and sprightly, talking to Oscar, to Mr January, Miss May and Mr November, far across their table. *I've lost her. For the second time in my life, I've lost her.* There was a moment when they were lying on the rock together like the most intimate of lovers, friends, sister-souls. He knew that she'd felt it as well, that moment. But life can take the most perfect day and ruin it. If life doesn't do it, then we'll be the ones to do it. This now, he could tell, was indeed ruined.

On her way out of the dining area she passed by his table and stopped short right by the chair where she'd sat during lunch. With her he didn't want to know anything or anticipate what she was going to say. He wanted her to sit at his table and pick up where they'd left off at lunch. Instead, she just stood before him, even placed a hand on the tablecloth, but said nothing. She looked so pinched that he knew she was mulling over how to strafe him with a volley of cutting words.

But she wasn't saying anything: she was waiting for the others to leave the area before talking to him; but even after they'd left she still wasn't speaking. He simply looked up at her beautiful face; he too had nothing to say. 'You could have warned me about the car that night, you could have warned me. Why didn't you?'

'Because I didn't believe it could happen. Because I thought I was being unreasonably paranoid. Because I just didn't want to think of it.'

'You didn't want to think of it. That's some gem, Raúl.'

She tapped her knuckles on his table twice as if to nail her point home. But she wasn't leaving yet. 'And for your information,' she added, 'I still remember the accident. I remember the sound in the car and the sound of the bones breaking in my body, and I remember not dying right away, too.'

He sat silent.

'Oh, and one more thing,' she added. 'It was not the road, not the fog, not the swirling eddies of rain that kept buffeting the hood of our car. Your driver was drunk, you hired a drunk driver. Why hadn't you told me?'

'I wish I'd died with you in the same car,' he said. 'We'd have been spared all this. Now we have to wait.'

'Oh please!' With that she hurriedly pulled on her windbreaker and, hearing the call of her friends who had ordered three cars, was about to walk out when she turned back to Raúl. 'So tell me now, should I get in the car, you think?'

He smiled at her. 'Yes, it's safe.'

'Goodnight, then.'

'Goodnight,' he echoed. He didn't quite under-stand what she'd meant by asking about the ride.

Was she pulling his leg and making light of his prophetic powers? He wasn't even able to interpret the word *then* that she'd just used. Was it an amic-able, conciliatory *then* that came like a friendly nudge of the elbow after strong words? Or did it underscore the chill, ironic cloud between them, and, as always with her, something unavoidably hostile and dismissive?

She had left the dining hall with peremptory haste, but a few moments later she returned. 'And one more thing: if you had anything to do with our boat, maybe it's time you released it.'

She had given everything he'd said a great deal of thought. That bit about their boat, which he'd thrown in as an afterthought when talking about kidney stones and back pains, hadn't escaped her. *So, you understand everything then*, he thought of saying to her. He heard the cars leave the hotel and feared he'd never see her again.

That night, he did what he'd done so many nights before. He took out a cigar, found himself a chair and a table, ordered a strong drink, and sat down and smoked. Nothing to read – he didn't really want to be distracted; nothing to listen to – music would blur his thoughts. He just wanted to think of the young man who'd entered a girl's room in his bathing suit and sat there, waiting for her to wake up and share the warmth of her body.

The cigar took forever to smoke. Then, at some point, he decided to stub it out, finished his drink, and opted for a walk along the shore. He left his glasses on the table, removed his shoes, rolled his trousers and proceeded to walk to the beach. Isn't this what those who are about to take their own lives do when they leave a note in their shoes on the edge of a bridge? Why on earth do people remove their shoes but not their socks, he thought, and what about their wallets, their watch – why punish a watch that stayed loyal to you all life long?

It made him want to laugh. He heard himself snickering.

What he couldn't quite fathom was why she always became so angry the closer he got to the truth. The more he convinced her she was Marya, the more she bristled. The violin was hers, so why hadn't she taken it, now that she knew he hadn't lied, now that she recalled the accident, recalled the sound of the car tumbling down, with the sound of her body breaking, and the drunk driver whose body, so they said, fell not just out of the car but down into the sea never to be recovered again. *Se l'hanno mangiato i pesci*, the fish ate him, they said.

But he couldn't let go of the moment when she had come up to his table, placed a palm on the tablecloth and asked why he hadn't warned her of the accident, as if it had all been his fault, and to bring the point home, had rapped the table twice. He'd never forget that gesture, followed by a smiling *then*, as if she'd meant no harm, as if peace were never in doubt between them, as if war and peace were, in the end, identical bedfellows.

Then there was that other instant, when she had swum with him to the rock and he had helped her up there with him. What a beautiful moment – one to make the gods envious.

Of course they were envious.

That night, the walk on the shore took him to the spot where the old lighthouse used to stand. He saw it now not as he remembered or as Alberti had captured it less than a decade after the war, but as she had described it: *a squat little hut made of stacked boulders with a strange round attic-looking structure from which scant light emanated to warn mariners of rocks and shoals.* Her words. Exactly as in the photo.

Later, when he was back in his room, a strange thought kept buzzing in his mind. He was pleased that they had spent time together, yet, on second thoughts, now that they'd been together, there was little left for him to do. He had waited so long for this, and now it had come and gone – come and gone, he repeated to himself.

Come and gone, he whispered out the words to himself as he brushed his teeth a while later, come and gone, as he read a few pages before sensing he was about to doze off, come and gone, when he was finally about to turn off his bedside light and thought about his own life that had come six decades ago and would soon be gone – and why not, he thought. And why not.

Then he heard the knock at his door. *I knew it, I've always known*, he thought.

'Come in.'

She was dressed in exactly the clothes he remembered her wearing when she'd stood before him and placed a hand on his table. Same blouse, same sweater, same necklace, same way she'd arranged her hair. Only her lipstick had faded.

'Finish the story,' she said, removing her linen shawl and sitting on the armchair that was close to his bed. He made a motion to turn on the main light in the room, but she told him not to.

'The story,' he said, with a melancholy smile. 'They wouldn't let me see the body. A few days later they wanted to take away her things and her clothes, but I didn't let them.

'Everything in her room stayed the way she left it. When I revisit the town, I always make a point of going upstairs and stepping into her room; I'll sit on her bed, think of her. There were times when I've flown all the way from Peru to sleep in her bed. Those are the only times in my life when I sleep ever so soundly. Sometimes I speak to her, sometimes I imagine what she'd say. "I've grown so old," I'll say. "Yes, you've grown old, and you do look old, my dear, dear man," she replies. And I'll ask her if she remembers the rock, or the cut on her wrist, or the sewing machine, and she'll say she still does, of course she does. And yet we never used the word love.'

'Why is that?'

'Maybe because it was more than just love, or maybe it was something else. But it never went away and I don't want it to. Still today, that one sentence she spoke to me some forty years ago – *Were you planning to swim in my bedroom?* – brings a smile to my life.'

Raúl couldn't see her, she sat slightly behind

him, and he liked it that way. There was a moment, given the silence that suddenly hovered between them, when he felt that perhaps she had already slipped away and left his room, or had never even been there.

'Why did you come tonight?' he asked.

'Because you wanted me to. Because I really didn't want us to drift away. Because I could tell you weren't happy, especially after such a lovely day.'

'So now we read minds?'

'I had a good teacher. But finish the story,' she said, tucking both feet under her thighs on the armchair that was so close to his bed.

He told her that he'd always kept an eye on her as she was growing up, had tried not to intrude, but knew where she lived, which school she attended, what college she was applying to, who were her friends and roommates. He kept hoping she'd pick up the violin, but she never did. 'And, honestly, part of me was waiting for you to get older.'

'Older than Marya?'

'Yes, otherwise I doubt you'd have spoken to me, much less had lunch with me.'

She shook her head lightly, as if to reproach him for something she had no words for, so just the gesture would do.

'Why not let go of me, forget, let the whole thing just go?'

'Can I now, especially after today? Can you?'

'I'm going to try.'

'Don't you think I've tried? Do you have any idea how happy you've made me? Mine wasn't bereavement. I wasn't in mourning. I wasn't even sad you died. I was just missing half my body, half my life, maybe all of it. I ended up living another man's life, not mine. I was no longer me. And yet I was a master at faking it with everyone. For years, each time I was alone – in the shower, or getting dressed, or in bed when I was alone in bed, or in the kitchen cutting up vegetables by myself on a Sunday evening – I'd mutter your name, *Mar-a-ya*, out loud and feel completely ridiculous doing so, and yet I was still happy that this name had come into my life, that I could call it, and by calling it even talk to it, as I'm talking to you now. At some point I realized that I just had to see you. Not to relive what had happened four decades before. All I wanted was to have you with me, for an hour, for a day – more I never dreamed of asking.'

'And?'

'I could have waited more time, as I'd been doing for so long, letting another five weeks, five months, five years go by. But my time's almost up, and this now is the hardest part for me, telling you what lies in store for me. For me the matter will be settled soon enough. I laugh at what awaits me: new parents, new schooling, new siblings, and the years and years of our crossing paths and never stopping, or occasionally turning back to catch a second glimpse only to let go because it's not our time, not our time yet, never our time.'

'How many years, Raúl?'

This was the first time she'd used his name. It pleased him and it moved him.

'How many? I don't want to tell you.'

'Why not?'

'Too many.'

'Just tell me.'

He hesitated for a moment.

'Three hundred and twenty-four. Eighteen times eighteen years.'

'Will we keep missing each other?'

'One day, when you're old and grey, you'll see a young man step out of a car, or walk up to your hotel lobby or enter a concert hall and you'll say, I know him, he's the man I met years ago at that hotel in southern Italy who kept telling me he'd known me another lifetime ago. It will be the young man in the picture, which is why I wanted you to keep it. I too will again and again run into you, but I'll be too old or too young, or you'll be too old or too young. But that day will come, I promise, though I have no vision of what our planet will be like.'

'I hate goodbyes, especially after today. You make me fear the years of loneliness awaiting me. Or worse yet, that my life and eighteen generations of my life will mean nothing. What do I do with these lifetimes? No one can wait this long.'

'We are all of us condemned to loneliness, each and every one of us. You died alone. I'll die alone. You yelled my name when the car fell, I call out yours each and every night of my life. At some point fate will realign our calendars and, if we're lucky, we'll live seventy long years together and then never again.'

He knew he was tearing up and so he stopped talking.

'Any idea what a privilege it was to have you for two lunches, to walk with you in the sun, to swim with you and let myself dream I was a young man again, eating fruit on the rock by the old lighthouse that isn't even there any longer?'

'What had you hoped might happen to us?' she asked.

'Nothing. I wanted you to love the young man I once was. I wanted you to look at me and tell me that you'd forgotten nothing, that you'd suffered for forty-plus years without knowing you were suffering, that you couldn't have been more grateful I'd brought you back here.'

'Did you really have something to do with the boat?' she asked.

'Yes,' he replied.

'Will you let it go?'

'When do you want me to?'

'Friday. This gives us two days.'

'Two more lunches, two more walks to our beach, the rock, maybe the house again.' Then he asked, because he had to ask: 'Will you be on the boat when I let it go?'

'I don't know. Yes. No. I don't know.'

'You will have to be. But tomorrow, very early, I'd planned a small errand for us.'

'An errand?'

'I want to take you to the cemetery. I want you to see her grave. And, as in the poem, we'll bring a nosegay of green holly and heather blossom.'

'Because?'

'Because it will be my way of closing the circle. At the very last minute you will go back with your friends and perhaps not believe a word of what happened here and, looking back, call the whole thing an old man's bluff, an old man's fiction. But seeing the grave will etch me forever in your heart. I've loved only you and will continue to love you long, long after I'm gone. In the years to come I want you to return, most likely, with your husband, your children, or come alone – yes, come alone. I don't have descendants, so the house will be yours. I signed the deeds three days ago. Only promise me one thing. Bury me near her.'

He turned to her. 'Aren't you cold?' he finally asked.

'Freezing,' she replied.

He remembered that word.

He'd waited a lifetime to hear her say it.